Raced

BOOK FOUR

K. BROMBERG

Cover art created by **Tugboat Design**
Copyediting by **Maxann Dobson of The Polished Pen**
Formatting by: **Champagne Formats**

Except for the original material written by the author, all songs, song titles, and lyrics mentioned in the novel Driven are the property of the respective songwriters and copyright holders.

ISBN: 9781682307816

Also by K. Bromberg

The Driven Series
Driven
Fueled
Crashed
Raced (Driven reading companion)
Aced

Driven Novels
SLOW BURN
SWEET ACHE
DOWN SHIFT

UnRaveled

Dedication

To my readers …

You are the *checkered* in my flag and complete my alphabet, *A to Z*.
　　You've given me the *rain to dance in* and the voice to *quack* with.
　　Your endless support, continued enthusiasm, and unwavering faith in my abilities overwhelm me on a daily basis.

　　This is the book I never intended to write, but you guys can be quite convincing … so this one is for you.

　　I race you. I book you. I chocolate you. I thank you.

Kristy

Foreword

When I started this journey, I had no intention of writing any part of these books in Colton's point of view. *Rylee was my girl*. I knew how she thought, plotted out her motivation from one scene to the next, and understood her resistance yet draw to the egotistical mess of a man that is Colton Donavan.

Not once did I contemplate what Colton was thinking other than why he would push her away.

All of the books I'd been reading were from the first person female point of view. I connected with the heroine this way, related to her actions, and that's what I set out to do for the readers when I wrote DRIVEN.

When DRIVEN was released, a blog commented in their review that they'd love to see some of the scenes through Colton's eyes because he was so complex. I struggled with the criticism, not because it was invalid but rather quite the opposite. The reviewer was spot on in saying this, but hell, I'd never written from a guy's perspective before. The thought scared the crap out of me.

I decided to challenge myself. I reached out to the blog and asked if they wanted a Colton point of view as an extra for their site. They accepted. And then I realized how lost I was because yes, I knew the dialogue that would take place, but not once did I ever question Colton's thoughts.

So writing the scene was rough going at first. I had to find his internal voice, his personality. And after days of type, delete, type, delete, *repeat*, I was finally finished.

And it was in that moment I realized I loved Colton even more than I thought I did. I loved his tell-it-like-it-is nature, his sarcasm, and better understood the demons that haunted him. There was something so liberating writing the scene through his eyes. I loved the challenge, enjoyed figuring out how his mind worked, and loved stepping outside of the story and looking at it with fresh eyes and in a totally different perspective.

Feedback was positive on the scene when the blog posted it. I looked at FUELED, which was about eighty percent complete and all in Rylee's point of view, and decided I needed to write some chapters from Colton's perspective. After the ending of DRIVEN, I figured the only way to get him back in the good graces of readers was to tell that last chapter through his eyes. I wanted readers to understand him so they could forgive him a little more.

I sat down and wrote the prologue of FUELED in one sitting. That had never happened to me before. But when I was done, I knew I was going to be ripping apart eighty percent of the book I had completed so I could add in more of Colton's voice.

In both FUELED and CRASHED, I was selective in the scenes I told from his perspective. I never wanted to give away too much or too little and always wanted his scenes to pack a punch, serve a purpose, but it never seemed like there were enough in the readers' eyes. I was (and still am) messaged constantly, and asked what he was thinking in this or that scene. I debated the idea of rewriting the series through his eyes but thought maybe his humor, his draw, would lose its luster to readers. That they'd become bored with a story they knew all the ins-and-outs of already.

But I did think certain events would still hold merit if retold, so I asked you guys, my readers, which scenes those were. Not surprisingly, many of them were the same as the ones I wanted to write.

So here they are, the Colton Points of View. A few are revamped versions of ones you may have read previously on a blog, some are new chapters retold, and some are scenes you've never read before because we saw what Rylee was doing but never knew what Colton was doing.

I hope you enjoy them, I know I did writing them. It was fun getting back into his complex and humorous mind, experiencing him conquer his demons, and watching him learn how to race blindly off the track.

DRIVEN BY NEED,
FUELED WITH DESIRE

Driven

BOOK ONE

K. BROMBERG

NEW YORK TIMES BESTSELLING AUTHOR

Driven

Chapter One

Many readers were curious what Colton thought during his first meeting with Rylee when she fell out of the storage closet. I was curious too; the problem was I had no idea. I didn't even know why he was wandering backstage in the first place.

This scene was my first attempt at writing Colton's point of view.

I started it at least seven times, trying to figure his motivation for heading farther away from the gala rather than being in the middle of it. The scene took me a long time to write but I'll forever look at it as the one that changed FUELED's direction ... for the better.

WHAT. THE. FUCK?

My body jolts with the impact as she slams into me. Fingernails dig into my biceps. A pile of wild, brown curls is all I see when I look down at the top of her head. Her shoulders shudder with each hyperventilated breath—a sound that goes hand in hand with the earsplitting scream that will inevitably happen next.

Thank you social media! You can take your goddamn tweets and stalker.com posts and shove them up your asses. Thanks for helping another faceless, frantic, fangirl find me.

What the fuck is it with women attacking me in this place? First the auburn piranha in the alcove and now this.

Seriously? The damsel in distress route? Like I haven't seen that one before. *You're one of millions, sweetheart.* You want me to notice you, baby, you've got to have less clothes on. Well, unless you count thigh highs and heels. And *nothing else.* That'd sure as hell catch my attention.

I shift my feet but she doesn't move. Okay, *stalker girl*, time's up. Let the fuck go so I don't have to be a dick and pry you off of—

Fuck me running.

The air punches from my lungs when her eyes—fucking magnificent eyes—look up at me from beneath dark lashes. Her head is still angled down so my only focal point is their unique bluish-purple color. Even with that crap smudged under them, the way she looks at me—shocked, terrified, relieved, all at once—stops the crass send-off from spewing out of my mouth.

What the fuck is wrong with me? Hysterics plus female equals crazy. A surefire sign to get the fuck away from her. Lesson learned a long ass time ago. She smells damn good, though. Focus Donavan, remember rule number one: *Don't ever dip the wick in the pool of crazies.*

Her eyes break from mine, gaze slowly descending, and stop on my lips again, silently staring. Her body stiffens, fingers tensing on my arms, breath stopping momentarily before shuddering out in a fortifying sigh.

Wait for it. Wait for it. It's coming. Her inevitable offer. The scripted rush of air and waste of breath where she tempts me with the wicked things she'll let me do to her body in exchange for the bragging rights of spending a few hours with me.

Been there done that, sweetheart. *Hence, rule number one.* Shit—she can toss the salad any way she wants, it doesn't mean that I'm gonna like the dressing.

She shifts onto her heels and stumbles further into me, firm tits pushing against my chest before jumping back like she's touched a livewire.

That's right, sweetheart, I'm electric.

It's the first time I get a glimpse of all of her, and she's definitely worth a second glance. She's got more curves than I'm used to but fuck if she doesn't wear them well. My eyes devour and take in the come-fuck-me heels, long, shapely legs, and the full, more than a handful-sized tits. And I've got big hands. I can't help the quickening of my pulse. She might be crazy, *but shit*, fangirl has one smoking hot body.

I don't hear the apology she fumbles through—her lame excuse why she was *trapped*—because my eyes travel further up and fixate on her mouth. *Sweet Christ*—perfect fucking lips. Now *those lips* I can picture just how perfect they'd look wrapped around my cock. It takes everything I have to not groan aloud at the image in my head of fangirl kneeling before me, *those* eyes looking up at me, and her cheeks hollowing as my dick slides in and out of her mouth.

Fuck this. Since when have I ever followed the goddamn rules?

Ha. Rule breaker, heartbreaker. I'll gladly take the title in exchange for a moment of fun with her.

Buh-bye rule number one.

I force myself to look away from her mouth and drag my gaze up to gauge the intention in hers. So she wants a wild night with the notorious bad boy? After the self-imagined porno I've just created in my head with her as the star, fuck if I won't give it to her.

But I'm going to make her work for it. Shit, what I've got is too good to give away for free. Fangirls are a dime a dozen, but I'm a fucking two dollar bill.

She averts her eyes again, and I watch them wander. *Yeah, she likes what she sees all right* ... I don't think she has any idea who she's up against.

Undoubtedly like a good a stalker should, she's read the rags and thinks this is going to be easy—that I sleep with anyone who spreads their legs for me. *She so wants to play.* Little does she know, I'm in the mood for a good game of hardball.

She just keeps staring, and I can't help the smile that curls one side of my mouth. Her eyes widen and her breath hitches. *Oh yeah,* she's definitely game. Talk about swinging for the fences.

After a beat, she drags her eyes back up to mine. Dilated pupils, parted lips, a flush creeping into her cheeks. *Fuck,* I bet that's how she looks when she's coming. My dick stirs at the thought of being the one to put that look on her face as I slide into the prize between her thighs.

Then walk away from her. What is it they say? Easy come, easy go.

"No apologies needed," I tell her, smirking at how this boring event just became a helluva lot more interesting. *Batter up.* "I'm used to women falling at my feet."

Her head snaps up and confusion mixed with what I'm guessing is disgust flashes through those extraordinary eyes of hers.

Welcome to the big leagues, sweetheart!

She opens her mouth again. Flustered. Stumbling over her words. I make her nervous. *Good.*

"Thanks. Thank you. The-the door shut behind me. It jammed. I panicked—"

When she speaks this time, I actually *hear* her voice. The telephone-sex operator rasp of it. *Shit.* My dick's doing more than stirring now. The sex-kitten purr is enough to make a monk hard. "Are you okay? Miss—?"

She just stares at me. Frozen. Indecision and confusion warring across her incredible features. She's questioning her resolve already? *Not a chance in hell.* She's not going anywhere. I always finish what I start, and this—the chance to hear her screaming my name while I'm buried in her later—is by no means over.

Game. On.

I reach out, cup the back of her neck, and pull her closer to me. That's all I plan on doing. A little touch to up the ante—force her to place her cards on the table or call her bluff. I pull her close enough to touch her lips, tease her a bit to let her know the stakes behind this unexpected game we're playing.

But fuck if I know what it is about her—something different, challenge or not—that's got me reaching my free hand out and running it up her arm, across the curve of her neck, and over her cheek.

I don't want to want her. Don't need her. Shit, a simple text will have Raquel in my bed in a heartbeat for a nightcap. Fuck, she's probably already there. Our arrangement may be nearing its end, but she's still game.

And she has mad skills.

But there's something about crazy fangirl that has me looking twice, has me forgetting this is a game.

Those eyes. Those curls, wild and fallen from her clip, looking like they've been fucked loose. Those plump, perfectly parted lips. *Sweet Christ*. I just might have to let her win this game because damn, she's not playing fair.

Options of how to play her flicker through my head. Dive right in and consider the consequences later or draw this out and have some fun with her?

Then she sucks in a ragged breath that let's me know she's affected. Let's me know she's bitten off more than she can chew. Hints at that little bit of vulnerability I see flicker in her eyes. And that sound—the subtle shudder telling me her body wants to betray her mind's warning to steer clear of me—is such a fucking turn on.

And desire overwhelms all logic.

Testosterone wins.

Just a little taste.

"Oh fuck it!" I slant my mouth over hers and use her surprised gasp to slip my tongue between her now parted lips. To taste what she's offering. *Holy shit!* Talk about knocking me off of my stride. The woman tastes like nothing I've ever had before. You hear addicts say that their first line of coke is what hooks them, causes them to do irrational things for the next fix. I finally get it.

Sweet. Innocent. Sexy. Willing.

Fuckin' A.

And before I can take more of what I suddenly want very badly, game be damned, she struggles and breaks her lips from mine.

Only one thought fills my head. Clouds my resolve.

More.

Her pulse quickens beneath my palm. Her panted breaths mix with mine. Her eyes flash with confusion and fear. And desire.

More.

"Decide, sweetheart," I demand, an unbidden ache settling deep in my balls and taking hold. "A man only has so much restraint."

Her eyes, so much contradiction flashes through them; they say "come fuck me" and "stay the fuck away" at the same time. Her lips part and then close. Her hands fist my lapel, indecision warring across her stunning features. Why the sudden resistance when she's getting exactly what she came here looking for? Did the stakes just become too real for her? *Ah … a boyfriend then.* How can she not have one when she looks like that?

She just stares at me, eyes blank but body still responding, as every nerve within me shouts to drag her against me and take until I get my fill of her addictive taste. Time's up, sweetheart. Decision's mine now. I'll show her what she wants. Give her what the boyfriend doesn't. She had her chance to walk away and she didn't. I sure as hell am not. I always get what I want.

And right now, I want her.

I tighten my fingers on her neck, unable to hold back the smile on my lips as I think about pressing into her soft curves and wet pussy. And then I move. She resists as I claim her mouth. I'm skilled but far from gentle as I coax her trembling lips open and take my next fix.

One more taste.

That's all I want. I lick my tongue against hers. Probing. Tasting. Demanding.

Sweet fucking Jesus. That's the only thought I can manage when she begins to respond, our bodies connecting, her tongue playing with mine. Her hands move, fingernails scrape along my jaw, and fist in my hair. A fucking inferno burns its way down my spine and into my gut, a groan falling from my mouth as her body moves against my rock hard dick. Her soft yielding to my steel.

Every primal urge in my body begs to touch her, to claim her as mine. I drag one hand down the curved lines of her hips, our bodies vibrating with adrenaline and desire. I put one hand on her back pressing her into me, my cock against her stomach, my knee wedging between hers. She responds instantly, the Holy Grail between her thighs rubbing against my leg so I can feel her wet and wanting pussy through my slacks.

So fucking responsive. Her body just complies with the subtlest hints from mine, reacts to the slightest touch. Takes selflessly. Submits willingly.

God, I want to corrupt her.

And then she makes the softest, most erotic fucking sound I've ever heard. A gentle moan that begs and pleads and offers all at the same time.

And I'm decided. Consumed. Determined.

Fuck the game.

Mine.

I want her. Have to have her. I'm calling the shots now. Adrenaline hits me, coursing through me like the wave of the green flag.

I need to make her mine.

I nip her lower lip then lick away the sting. *Pleasure to bury the pain.* "Christ, I want you right now." I murmur against her lips between kisses, my dick throbbing at the thought of slamming into her. My hands move to possess now. Desire fueling my fire. Fingers rub over hardened nipples just begging to be tasted as we crash against the wall. My hands roam to connect with naked flesh. I reach the silk of her nylons and skim my way up until I trace the lace tops of her thigh-high stockings. I groan into her mouth.

Motherfucking perfection. Silk, lace, and skin. If it's possible to get any harder, I just did.

I guess fangirl doesn't want to be considered a dime a dozen.

As she gains confidence, her tongue taunts mine in a dizzying barrage of maneuvers. My fingertips snake up the bare skin of her inner thigh—smooth softness just pleading for me to lick, suck, and nip. I reach the swatch of lace at my awaiting heaven just begging to be ripped off.

"Sweet Jesus," I murmur as I feel how wet the material is, how ready she already is for me.

"No. No—I can't do this!" She pushes me back a step, and I watch her bring a trembling hand to her mouth. Her eyes tell me no, but her body? Her treacherous body vibrates with anticipation: chest heaving, lips swollen, nipples pebbled.

I force myself to swallow. To breathe. To regain the equilibrium she just shook and pulled out from under my always steady feet. I've had more women than any guy could ever ask for, but she just rocked my fucking world with her lips alone.

She's not going anywhere.

Mine.

"It's a little late, sweetheart. It looks as if you already have." *Like you have any fucking choice now.* You started this, fangirl, and I'll say when it's finished.

Fire leaps into her eyes and she lifts her chin in insolence. *My God,* that look alone gives new meaning to the word sexy.

"Who the hell do you think you are?" she spits at me. "Touching me like that? Taking advantage of me that way?"

We're back to the damsel in distress thing again? "Really?" I scoff at her, running my hand over my jaw as I ponder what to say next.

It's a little late for self-preservation, sweetheart.

"That's how you want to play this? Were you not participating just now? Were you not just coming apart in my arms?" I can't help the sliver of a laugh that escapes. "Don't fool your prim little self into thinking that you didn't enjoy that. That you don't want more."

I take a step closer and I can see a mixture of emotions flicker in her eyes. But most of all I see fear and denial. Resistance. Is she going to ignore what just happened between us? *Fangirl just might be crazy after all.* But fuck-all if I don't already crave my next taste of her.

And I have every intention of having it.

She watches as I lift my hand and trace a finger along the line of her cheek. Despite the hard set of her jaw, she instinctively moves her face ever so subtly in response to my touch. *Oh yeah.* She's definitely still interested, so why is she fighting it so hard?

"Let's get one thing clear," I warn through gritted teeth, trying to mask my irritation at having to fight for something that all of a sudden became complicated. "I. Do. Not. Take. What's. Not. Offered. And we both know, sweetheart, you offered. *Willingly.*"

She jerks her chin from my fingertips. Who knew defiance could be so goddamn arousing? And irritating. I can't remember the last time I had to work to get a woman beneath me.

Her body vibrates with anger. Or desire. Of which I can't tell. I step back into her personal space, pissed at myself that I've allowed her to affect me this much.

"That poor defenseless crap may work with your boyfriend who treats you like china on a shelf, fragile and nice to look at. Rarely used." I shrug as if I don't care, but all I want is a reaction out of her. Anything to tell me what she's thinking behind her stoic façade. "But admit it, sweetheart, that's boring."

"My boy—" she stutters, hurt flashing in her eyes. Hmm. She must have just broken up with him. Perfect time for a pump and dump, then. "I'm not fragile!"

Bingo!

"Really?" I want to push more buttons. Get her to admit she wants me. I reach out and grip her chin with my thumb and forefinger to make sure she can't hide from my stare. "*You sure act that way.*"

She jerks her chin from my hand as "Screw you!" grates from between her beautiful lips. The heat in her eyes holds me captive.

And to think I was going to pass up fangirl without a second thought.

"Oh, you're a feisty little thing!" I can't help the smirk on my lips. If she's this lively now, I can only image how wild she'll be between the sheets. "*I like feisty, sweetheart.* It only makes me want you that much more."

So many emotions pass over her face that I can't begin to comprehend them. She steps to the side of me, putting distance between us in our silent stand-off. Just as I think she's about to speak, the door down the hallway opens, flooding the quiet corridor with noise from the party beyond. Right before fangirl whirls around at the sound, I see a flicker of relief on her face.

I glance around her to see an average-sized guy standing with his back to the door, eying us with blatant curiosity. For a second I can't place him, but then realize I saw him earlier with some of the Corporate Care bigwigs. "Rylee? I really need those lists. Did you get them?"

Rylee? What the fuck?

"I got sidetracked," she mumbles to the guy as she glances back at me, her expression a mix of relief, regret, and disappointment. *She works with him? For Corporate Cares?* She says something else to the guy that I don't hear because I'm trying to wrap my head around the fact that crazy fangirl isn't a fangirl at all.

Or crazy.

Rylee. It sounds vaguely familiar. I mentally roll her name around on my tongue, liking the way it sounds, the way it feels.

She skirts past me and avoids making eye contact before stepping into the storage closet. I stop myself from reaching out for her because we're far from finished here. I follow her, hold the door open, and watch her jerky movements as she hurriedly shoves auction paddles into a bag. I can feel her co-worker's eyes boring holes in my back as he tries to assess the situation. Guaranteed he's telling me to *step off.*

The same way that I feel about him. Step off buddy so we can finish what we started here. I glance back to Rylee and she straightens up with the bag in hand, squares her shoulders, and walks past me without a second glance.

Anger fires in my veins. I do not get dismissed. "This conversation isn't over, Rylee."

"Like hell it isn't, Ace." She throws the words over her shoulder as she stalks down the corridor.

I watch her walk away. Hips swaying with purpose. Curves begging to be touched. Heels—heels I want left on with nothing else but those fucking lace top stockings—clicking against the floor.

Since when have I ever considered a woman walking away to be one of the hottest fucking sights I've ever seen?

The door closes behind them, and it's silent once again. I run a hand through my hair and lean back against the wall, trying to wrap my head around the past twenty minutes. I blow out a loud breath, confused as to why I'm pissed.

You must be losing your touch, Donavan.

Shit, when they walk away, it's supposed to be a good thing. Lessens the chance of complications. I don't chase. It's not my thing—never has been, never will be. There are too many willing women; why bother wasting my time on the ones that make things difficult? Why work for it when life's complicated enough as it is? I fuck who I want, when I want. My pick. On my terms. To my benefit. Rules two through six.

But shit … that … her … how can I just let her—Fuck me!

Nobody walks away until I say I'm done. And I have every intention of finishing what I started with her. Checkered flag's mine. I'll definitely be crossing that finish line.

Here's to a night of firsts.

First a brunette.

Next a pursuit.

Bring it on.

Raced

Wave that checkered flag, sweetie, because I'm gonna claim it.

Driven

Chapter Three and then some

As the reader, we assumed Colton had something to do with the rigging of the date auction. This assumption is one I will never divulge the truth to because I think it's important for each person to create their own scenario. Regardless, we know that Rylee's been auctioned off and she's not too happy about it. She's flustered, not thinking clearly, and just wants to go home.

As always though, her boys are front and center in her mind and that means she has to find the arrogant yet achingly handsome Donavan to collect her winnings from the bet. Little does she know the chain of events this meeting will trigger.

I enjoyed writing this scene. I knew Colton was arrogant, but what were his thoughts behind his comments? What happened after he walked away that night and went home? How did the wavy-haired, defiant-as-fuck woman affect him?

FUCK MY RULES.
Addictive.
Fuck her defiance.

She's mine.

She just doesn't know it yet.

My eyes collide with hers as she steps out of the backstage door. The sneer on her face and fire in her eyes tells me *she knows.*

But that's not possible.

She couldn't have figured it out yet. But I'll be damned if she's not pissed off by the way she's stalking those sexy-as-fuck curves toward me right now. I can't help my eyes as they drag over every inch of her body, wanting more than just the taste I got earlier. I want the whole fucking meal.

And I want it now.

Patience is definitely not my virtue.

And I'm sure as fuck going to steal hers.

I can't help the smile that threatens the corners of my lips as I push myself off of the wall when she nears. A freight train of anger and she doesn't even have a clue that I'm her fucking fuel.

What I wouldn't give to push her up against the wall and taste her again—crowd around us be damned—so long as I get my fix. She reaches up and holds her hand to stop me before I speak. Fuck! The woman does everything to try and turn me off, and all it does is spur me further the opposite way, arousing me like she wouldn't fucking believe.

"Look, Ace, I'm tired and in a really shitty mood right now. It's time for me to call it a night—"

"And just when I was going to offer to take you to places you didn't even know existed before." I can't help pushing her buttons. The words are out of my mouth before I can stop them. *But fuck if it's not true.* I have no doubt we'd set the sheets—if not the fucking bed or floor or couch or wherever we crash—on fire. Those luscious lips of hers fall lax at my comment, and I figure I'll keep her on her toes. Keep pushing those buttons. It's just too much goddamn fun. "You don't know what you're missing, sweetheart."

She snorts. She actually snorts at me standing here in her elegant dress, and fuck me if that too isn't a mix of sexy and adorable. "I'm wounded," I say, clutching my heart in mock pain. *"You'd be surprised what my mouth gets with those lines."*

Let's see what she says to that one. My eyes trace over the outline of those lips that I want wrapped around my cock, those fucking magnificent eyes looking at me with a trace of shock. Even after all of our interactions tonight, she still doesn't know how to take me.

Good. Keep her guessing. Confusion is my advantage.

"I don't have time for your childish games right now. I just had to endure humiliation beyond my worst nightmare, and I'm more pissed off than you can imagine. I *especially* don't want to deal with *you* right now."

"I do love a woman who tells it like it is," I murmur to myself, unable to tear my eyes from hers. Or comprehend being told no. That's a new one.

"So I'm going home in about ten minutes. Night's over. I win our idiotic bet, so you better get your check and fill it out because you're going home with lighter pockets tonight," she rants and places her hands on her hips.

Fuck, there's that defiance again that makes my balls tighten in anticipation. In unfettered lust. And she thinks I'm just going to write her a check and let her walk out of my life without having her? She's sadly mistaken. I'm a take it or leave it kind of guy.

And I'm definitely taking this one. Too bad she doesn't know it yet.

I don't fight my smirk this time. *Game on, baby.* "Twenty-five thousand lighter, in fact."

"No, we agreed on twen—" Her voice fades and I watch as it slowly hits her. The realization crashes like a tornado across her features and storms through her eyes. I can see her trying to fight it. Trying to resist the urge to throttle me.

And shit, if I thought defiance made her sexy, then anger makes her motherfucking breathtaking.

"No—uh-uh. This is bullshit and you know it!" She glares at me with every ounce of hatred I think she can muster, and it only makes me more determined to have her. "That wasn't the deal. I didn't agree to this!"

I tuck my tongue in my cheek, trying to bite back the grin tugging at the corners of my mouth. "A bet's a bet, Ryles."

"It's Rylee, you asshole!" she hisses at me.

Testy. Testy. *Ryles it is, then.*

"Last time I checked, sweetheart, my name wasn't *Ace.*" *But when you're screaming my name later, it can be anything you want it to be.* I lean back against the wall and watch the emotions play over her face.

She's so frustrated. Mission accomplished, buttons pushed. And now I have one feisty hellcat on my hands, and I bet sure as fuck she's going to be fun to try and tame. Then again, why tame her? A few scratches never hurt anyone.

"You cheated. You-you-aaarrgh!"

"We never had time to outline any rules or stipulations," I explain with a raise of my eyebrows and a shrug of my shoulders. "You were pulled away. That left everything as fair game."

Those lips of hers that I want to taste fall open and then close again to only fall back apart. I pull my thoughts from what else I'd like them to open and close around. *Sweet Christ!* I force my mind to focus on the here and now and away from what exactly is under that dress. I push myself off the wall and step toward her.

I can't resist.

"I guess I just proved you do in fact lose sometimes, *Ryles.*"

I have to touch her.

Irresistible.

Mine.

"I'm looking forward to our date, Rylee."

I watch her eyes follow my fingers as they move a loose curl of hair from her cheek. I catch the slight hitch in her breath, and I know I've got her. Know it's only a matter of time now.

The pull is just too great. Resistance is futile. I graze a thumb over her cheek, wanting to feel her skin. Needing to feel that spark of current that vibrates between us. "In fact, more than any other date I've had in a while."

She leans her head back, my thumb still on her cheek, and "Oh God!" falls from her mouth in exasperation.

The sound of her sex-kitten voice turns my insides, calls to some part deep within me, and I don't like it one bit. The only part of me that should be affected should be my dick and my mind counting the minutes until she's beneath me.

Or on top of me. Beggars can't be choosers and fuck if reverse cowgirl isn't a mighty nice position.

See, Donavan? It's the alcohol twisting things around making you think that feeling deep down is more than just the ache in your balls. C'mon, all you want is a quick, uncomplicated fuck and an attempt to tame the wildcat.

That's it. Nothing else.

I swear.

Unease creeps through me at the thought of only having her once, and I force myself to stop thinking this fucking nonsense and grab the control back my dick has hijacked. I hear those words of hers echo through my mind, and I know exactly how to do it.

"Those words, *oh God*," I mimic her and give in one last time to my need to touch her by running a finger down the side of her face. "Now I know exactly how you'll sound when you say that while I'm buried deep inside of you."

I love the look of shock that flashes across her face. Love the insolence in her expression as she lifts her chin and glares at me. Such a fucking turn on.

"Wow! You sure think a lot of yourself, don't you, Ace?"

Shit! She walked right into that one and I can't resist. Just can't fucking stop myself from pushing those buttons of hers one last time before I walk away and leave her wondering whose court the ball is really in. I slip my hands in my pocket and lean into her, the smile on my face suggesting exactly what I want to do with her. To her. For her.

"Oh, sweetheart, *there is definitely a lot of me to think about.*" I laugh softly, loving the look I've just put on her face. "I'll be in touch."

I forgo the urge to touch her one last time. Taste her one last time. And I force myself to turn around and walk away. To put one foot in front of the other when I'd much rather be dragging her back to that damn storage closet and taking exactly what I want.

The chance to claim her.

Game fucking on.

I walk out into the parking lot and thank fuck Sammy is already there or else I might be tempted to walk back inside. Because fuck yes her playing hard to get is a turn on, but experience has me wagering that given ten more minutes either I wouldn't be going home alone or that storage closet just might have gotten some use.

Can't say I have a losing track record.

I pull my phone from my pocket and laugh when I see the notifications blaring across my screen. Case in fucking point. I thumb through the ten texts from Raquel. Each one dirtier than the first.

Sweet Jesus I could use a good fuck tonight after all of that verbal foreplay and by the suggestions she's sent to my phone, it's gonna be a long, sweaty, sleepless night.

"Hey, Wood. Good night?" Sammy asks as I climb into the back of the Range Rover, fingers already untying my bowtie and undoing the noose of buttons closing my collar on my neck.

"You have no idea, Sammy," I tell him and then laugh when my thoughts veer to how my evening has turned into the beginning of a good joke—*so a redhead, a brunette, and a blonde walk in a bar*—when I think of Bailey, Rylee, and Raquel.

He laughs and shakes his head, having been with me long enough that he knows how my life goes. Women willing for whatever I'm game for. Well except for the unexpected Ms. Thomas tonight.

Knowing what was beneath that dress has made it ten times harder to walk away without having her. Since when do I care what a woman's wearing so long as it's piled on the floor?

Normally I'd say she's not worth my time, but I can't remember the last time I had a challenge. Shit, women say the word no to me about as often as they keep their legs together at the knees. *Never.*

Christ, I should let it go. Write the check, Donavan. Leave her alone.

Don't touch complicated—that's my default. So why in the fuck do I want to play with fire? Light the match to her flame and see how hot she gets.

Damn it to Hell.

I'm just horny. Pump primed and turned on from her defiance. I'll lose myself in Raquel tonight—every tight fucking inch of her—and realize I'm being stupid. That I shouldn't opt for complicated when I can have easy.

Decision made. Mind-numbing sex. That fixes everything.

I'm just about to text Raquel back when my phone rings. I look down to see her name. Well, can't get much easier than that.

Damn, I'm good. All that's missing is the snap of my fingers

"Hey." I smirk at Sammy meeting my eyes in the rearview mirror.

"I'm naked. I'm wet. And my mouth is ready to suck your cock 'til you're dry. I sure hope you're coming home soon because my mouth is kind of empty and, baby, I'd love for you to fill it."

My dick is already stirring to life, balls tightening. The need to come front and center. What red-blooded male wouldn't be with that greeting? Shit.

"Fuck, baby, that sounds like Heaven … but I need to take a rain check." My own words shock me. *What the fuck are you doing, Donavan? What is wrong with you?* I hear myself yelling, my dick begging, but my mouth has a mind of its own.

"What?" Her voice is soft, disappointment evident.

"I'm sorry. My mom needs me to stay here and wrap up some of the charity shit for her. I'll make it up to you, though. I was invited to some launch party for the new sponsor, Merit Rum. It'd be good exposure for you—media and big wigs and shit, okay? You know I wouldn't pass up the chance to fuck you unless it was unavoidable."

I just used my mother to get out of fucking Raquel. There is something extremely pathetic about my state of mind right now. Is the Apocalypse coming? Is Hell freezing over?

What. The. Fuck?

She accepts reluctantly, I apologize again, lie about being busy, and end the call. Sammy catches my eyes and just raises his eyebrows. "I take it I should drive to Broadbeach instead, now?"

I scrub a hand through my hair and sigh. "Yeah." I shake my head trying to figure out what in the fuck I just did. "Sammy, did I just pass up pussy?"

"Yep. Sounded like it. You feeling okay? Dick still attached? It didn't fall off with all of the hobnobbing at the event?"

Fucking Sammy. Dude's funny as hell. I grab my dick and adjust it. "Still there, Sam. Still there." My voice trails off as my thoughts wander.

Rylee Thomas. It's gotta be because of her. How could three fucking hours of defiance make me look at wet and willing and think it's too damn easy? That working for a piece of ass might be fun for a change.

It's her fucking fault I'm headed home to my hand and some lube. And even I know it's fucked up so I start to tell Sammy to head

18

to the Palisades but nothing comes out of my mouth. Because as hot as Raquel is and as good as she can ride me, my interest is elsewhere.

Back at the benefit. With curves and class and holy fuck that ass of hers. And that's just scratching the surface of everything I plan on touching.

My phone rings again and I'm immediately irritated. Raquel needs to drop it and leave me the hell alone. "What?" I bark the word into the phone, Sammy's shoulders moving as he laughs at my self-inflicted misery.

"Wow. Someone needs to get laid. Relieve stress and shit." Shit. Guess I should have looked at the screen. I was so lost in what I can't have right now that I assumed it was Raquel and not Becks.

"Sorry," I tell him. "I thought you were Raquel."

"Damn, dude." He laughs. "I guess she's holding out on you tonight by the pissiness in your tone. She make other plans or something besides being at your beck and call?"

Fucker. I grunt out a laugh. "Hardly. Just not on the menu tonight."

Becks chokes out a cough on the other end of the line. *Fuck,* I just left him an open door to walk right through. "Well considering your menu is usually pussy pie, I guess you're looking for a new diner to eat it out of besides Raquel."

The smile is wide on my face but my silence tells him volumes.

"*Who'd you meet, Wood?*" I can hear the *here we go again* in his voice and just shake my head because he's right. "What woman has made you look at Raquel like she's an inconsequential notch in that belt of yours?"

The only belt notch I'm thinking of is mine coming undone so I can take Rylee beneath me and hear that *oh God* fall from her mouth. My head fills of lace-top thigh-highs, her smart-assed mouth, and violet eyes filled with contempt. Two of the three should turn me off but fuck if it doesn't make my dick jerk thinking of the whole fucking package.

"Nobody." I lie to protect myself from the one thing I fear the most.

That Rylee just might be the somebody I told myself I'll never allow myself to have.

She's a forever kind of girl and I'm a just for the night kind of guy.

But fuck if it's not going to be fun to see just how far we'll each bend to break our own rules.

Driven

Chapter Eleven

The Merit Rum launch party. Need I say more? A long-standing request from readers is what was Colton thinking that night? The following is Chapter Eleven from the moment Colton saw Rylee with Surfer Joe snuggling up against her until he asked her that now familiar line: "Decide, Rylee. *Yes. Or. No.*"

There's something about Colton in the hallway, his inner-monologue that intrigued me. He seems to always be in a constant struggle—denying himself what he wants, rationalizing he can have it but on certain terms, mixed with the side of him wanting to protect Rylee from the hurt he knows he is going to cause. All three pull at your heart strings for certain reasons while at the same time cause you to wear a neck brace to protect you from the whiplash of his emotions and his actions.

Uh-uh. She's mine, motherfucker.

Over my dead fucking body.

Or most likely *his* if he touches her again.

This club is so packed. So filled with more than willing Grade

A pussy. *And sponsorship obligations.* Fucking obligations that have weighed me down like an anchor for the past two hours. Two hours wasted when I could have been with the cause of my shitty mood.

And the source of my current case of raging blue balls.

Sweet Jesus. Dancing with her like that? Pressed against each other from shoulder to knee. Moving in sync. Her body reacting to mine as if she knew each movement I would make before I did. Eyes telling me she's mine for the taking.

The hint of how we'll be together when she finally caves to what her body wants but that her mind keeps fighting. I almost came on the spot. Talk about a tease I can't wait to devour.

And now I have Merit Rum execs in front of me, Raquel plastered to my side making it unmistakable to everyone that she's my date, and Becks, *the bastard,* over their shoulders smirking at me like *it's your fucking fault for asking her to come tonight.*

But more importantly is what I can see through the crowd in interrupted bouts. The man who just sat next to Rylee. Whose arm is around her shoulders. Who is leaning into her, speaking in her ear.

Mine.

The thought snags in my mind and I can't let it go. Let the thought of her go. I can't concentrate on what's being said. I look at the execs from Merit trying to act cool but failing miserably in an element they're obviously uncomfortable in. I glance up at Becks and nod to the side in Rylee's direction hoping he gets my drift and if he doesn't, he will in about five seconds.

"If you'll excuse me," I interrupt the shorter one's spiel about market demographics, "I need to use the restroom." I look again at Beckett, the *greatest fucking wingman ever,* and leave without another word. I just hope they don't realize I'm walking the opposite direction of the head.

What the fuck am I doing? Blowing off a sponsor for a chick? She must have the elusive voodoo pussy or something. *Fucking Christ!* It's like someone has taken over my body—or my dick—because once again I can't get her out of my goddamn system.

And I have to. There's no other option. No other choice. Have to finish the fucking meal I've had just a taste of right before it's cruelly snagged away.

The fucker is touching her. *Again.* Leaning closer.

"The lady's with me." The words are out before I can think. Grated out between my gritted teeth. My voice laced with the obvious threat. All four heads in the booth snap up at my comment and look at me. All except for Rylee. She stares at the blonde who works at PRX sitting across from her for a split second.

And then she turns ever so slowly against the chest of the prick sitting behind her, her posture stiffening with that defiance that causes my balls to tighten with unfiltered lust. Gone is the sexy siren from the dance floor earlier and the vulnerable girl from last night. Right now she's a woman scorned. And when she raises those eyes, I can see it clear as day, but I don't care because they are looking exactly where they need to be.

On me.

The only place I want them to be. But all I can focus on is him. His arm is still on her. His body still beside hers. I clench my jaw. Eyes locked with hers.

"I'm with you?" she asks, those fucking bedroom eyes widening to saucers and her chin jutting out in obstinance. "*Really?* Because I thought you were with her?" she says sarcastically, scrunching up her nose the way she does when she's pissed off—which I've happened to see a lot in the short time we've known each other—and looking behind me. "You know, the blonde from your arm earlier?"

Fucking Raquel. Why'd I invite her again? Her blowjob skills— her best asset frankly, *even if thinking it makes me a prick*—are a distant memory at the sight in front of me. Because right here, right now, all I can think of is Rylee. Her mouth. Her body. That pussy of hers that I'll bet my life on as being the sweetest fucking thing I'll ever taste. Ever feel.

Might even beg for.

I need to be buried in her so badly right now it's painful. "Cute, Rylee." I spit the words out, not trusting myself to say any more when I see Surfer Joe squeeze her shoulder. My glare shifts to his, my eyes sending the message.

Hands. Off.

I see that my warning's delivered when he tenses as recognition slowly seeps in. *Yeah, that's right, cocksucker. I'm Colton Fuckin' Dona-*

van and she's mine. And the exaggerations in the tabloids are perfectly accurate. I've got a quick fucking temper and have no qualms getting my hands dirty with a few punches. Touch her again and I'll show you.

Pretty please.

And of course because she always does the opposite of what I want, Rylee turns and puts her hand on the fucker and reassures him that she's not here with me. Then she turns back slowly to me, a derisive smirk on those beautiful lips and challenge in her violet eyes.

So that's how this is going to go?

"Don't push me, Rylee. I don't like sharing," I say, clenching and unclenching my fists to release the anger laced with arousal that's firing through my veins. "You. Belong. With. Me."

Her eyebrows shoot up at my claim. I can see the insolence just beneath her composed exterior. "How so, Ace? Last night you were with me, and tonight you're with *her.*" She says *her* like the meanest of slurs, and I can't help but think the same thing. I send a silent thanks to Becks for getting my hint and keeping Raquel occupied right now. "Seems to me like—She. Belongs. With. You." She mimics me.

Sweet Christ! *The woman fucking owns me.* Owns me and I haven't even had her yet. What the fuck is wrong with me? I never chase. Never. But the goddamn woman is constantly pulling me in two opposing extremes. I swear to God she's got some kind of fucking hold on me I can't break from.

I drag my hand through my hair in frustration as I take in the other three sitting in the booth, witness to the stringing of my balls by a singular woman. "Rylee." I sigh, trying to rein in the impatience in my voice. "You—you ..." *She's what, you dumbass?* Grab your balls back firmly and own them. Tell her how it's going to be. "You test me on every level. Push me away. What am I supposed to think?"

Yeah. That was brilliant, Donavan. Fucking brilliant, if you're a pussy.

She eyes me up and down, a little smirk at the corners of her mouth that irritates the fuck out of me. Makes my dick hard. She's playing me once again. Fucking toying with me.

And enjoying it.

"*I'm not sure if I want you yet,*" she antagonizes, startling everyone else at the table, I assume because of my rumored temper and unpredictability. "A girl's allowed to change her mind," she taunts, angling her head and deliberately looking me up and down. "We're notorious for it."

"Among other things." I shoot back instantly and then take a sip of my drink, watching her above the rim all the while. "Two can play this game, Ryles, and I think I have a lot more experience at it than you do."

Her lips part slightly at my words and I want to groan out loud at the fucking image that flickers through my head. Of exactly how I can fill that space between them. I grit my teeth in need as I level my stare at her. She slowly removes her hand from Surfer Joe's knee and scoots toward the edge of the booth.

Toward me.

That's right, sweetheart. Let's end this. Right here. Right now. Come to Daddy.

"You're playing hard to get, Rylee."

She glances over at her girlfriend and then slowly rises from her seat, and all I seeare her sweet curves and soft flesh and my head fills with thoughts of how desperately I want her beneath me, naked and coming undone. "And your point is ...?"

Her words force me to focus back to now. To winning her over, despite the combustible sexual chemistry between us that she's constantly fighting. But when I see her—hear her—her shoulders are proud with defiance and her chin, strong.

She wants to go this route? Keep up the charade that she doesn't want me despite her fucking unbelievable body announcing otherwise. I can play this like nobody's business. Run circles around her. I shake my head at her and take a step closer.

Needing to be closer.

She lowers her eyes under my intense scrutiny. "I hope you're enjoying yourself because it's quite a show you're putting on here." I reach out and force her chin up so she has no other option but to look me in the eyes. "I don't like games, Rylee," I warn, my blood thundering through my veins from being so close to her. "... and I won't tolerate them played on me."

The air thickens between us. My breath quickens. My fingers itch to touch.

To possess.

To claim.

She's just as fucking affected as I am. I know it. Can see it. *Fuck me.* The woman turns me inside out, and I can see the moment she tries to deny what's humming between us right now. She takes a slow, calculated breath and steps toward me. "Well, thanks for the update." She slaps her hand to my chest and leans into me, her lips right at my ear.

My senses riot. My restraint tested. The woman needs to back away right now or I'll take her right here on the damn floor. *No holds barred.*

"I'll let you in on a little something as well, Ace. I don't like being made to feel like sloppy seconds to your *blonde bevy of babes.*" Her voice tickles my skin. And she continues to tease as she takes a step back, that smile on her face tempting me to just take without asking. "You're developing a pattern of wanting me right after you've been with another. That's a habit you're going to need to break or nothing else is going to happen here." She gestures back and forth between us, my mind wandering to exactly what else she can do with that perfect-ly manicured hand. "... That's if I want it to at all."

She smirks at me as she retreats a step. *That smirk* that I'd like to fuck into submission until she's screaming out my name. And I've had enough of this banter. Desire's so strong in me that my balls ache. I'm just about to act on it. To take without asking when I hear "Colt, baby?" followed by a hand sliding up my torso to display ownership. I tense when all I really want to do is shrug Raquel off of me like a hot fucking coal.

The look on Rylee's face—her complete disdain for Raquel—I completely understand. I feel the same way at this exact moment. But what gets me more than anything is the flash of hurt that lingers in those violet eyes a moment too long.

Fuck! I knew it.

She wants this just as bad as I do. There's nothing I can do right now and not look like a dick. Drop Raquel and go after Rylee or leave Rylee after the game I just played and walk away with Raquel. I do the only thing I can do when all my mind and hands want to do is grab

Rylee against me and taste her mouth. Sample her body.

I toss back the rest of my drink, the burn of the alcohol not even registering. When I look back toward Rylee, she's saying something to her friend and then picks up her purse. She turns back to face me and my chest tightens. That defiance I find arousing is evident in her posture, but her eyes reflect a myriad of contradictions.

I hate you.

I want you.

How could you?

I should've known.

You're going to break my heart, aren't you?

Your choice: *me or her.*

I clench my jaw. Having answers to all of them. And none of them. She just looks at me one more time, a quiet resignation in her face, and then she turns and pushes her way through the crowd of people. Getting away from me as fast as she can.

I'd run too, sweetheart. That's nothing compared to the poison inside of me.

I look down at the empty glass in my hand while Raquel tugs on my arm, urging me to follow her. I resist the desire to huck it against the wall and hear the crash as the glass splinters into a thousand tiny fucking pieces.

What the fuck are you doing, Donavan? Since when do you care what people think? Fucking voodoo pussy, man. That's got to be it. Got to be the only reason I want to chase the one thing I've never wanted. Never cared to.

Until now.

Fuckin' A.

I look up and meet the blonde friend's eyes. She just arches her eyebrow at me as if to say *"You fucking idiot."* And she's right. *I am.*

I look over to Raquel. And feel nothing. Absolutely nothing. No buzz. No charge. No ache to take.

I look into the mass of people where Rylee left and I catch a glimpse of her head as she weaves through the crowd. My chest tightens. My fingers rub together. My body craves. And the need humming through me is so strong, all I can do is shake my head at Raquel. My eyes telling her the only words that need to be said.

And then I walk away.

There's not even a choice to be made.

It was made for me. The moment she fell out of that damn storage closet and into my life.

Fucking Rylee.

Fucking voodoo pussy.

The two thoughts are on repeat in my head as I push through the crowd to try and find where in the hell she went.

I'm annoyed I can't find her. Pissed because Colton Donavan does not chase and fuck if this woman hasn't had me on the run since the get-go.

It's easy to tell myself to let her go. Fuck the hassle. So why can't I?

I scan the crowd and through a break I see her at the bar. I push through, tell myself I'm chasing because of the challenge and from the need to show her that she wants this … even if it's just because she's so goddamn nonchalant about rejecting me.

Women aren't blasé when it comes to wanting me. She tried to be but I saw her nipples tighten through her top, her pulse beat in her throat. I know I affected her.

Blasé my ass. She's fucking lying and another shot, another drink, another woman isn't going to convince me otherwise.

I'm used to getting what I want and right now, I want this fucking woman more than any other.

I reach the bar and she catches sight of me, turns, and then hurries to the exit.

Fuckin' A. She's running again and I'm chasing.

And the thing about chasing in racing is sometimes it's a bitch to win a race from behind. But then again, chasing can let you draft, fly beneath the radar, and then slingshot to take the lead and control the race when it matters the most.

Time to slingshot.

I push through the exit moments after her. We're in some type of hallway but I don't take notice because our eyes lock. I see the hurt flash before she turns and keeps going.

Uh-uh. No way. She's not walking away from me again because I may have seen hurt, but I also saw something else. And I need to know what that something else is.

But why, Donavan? Why the fuck do you care when you can have any woman you want? Snap your fingers and another one will replace the current one?

I grit my teeth as I chase, the view of her walking away becoming a familiar one but hell if it's not hot as fuck to watch her ass sway. And therein lies the motherfucking problem. That view is what keeps me coming back for more. And I lie to myself again because I know it's so much more than just the curves that keep me chasing.

Let her go. Let her keep on walking out of the hallway, out of my life.

But I don't want her to. There's just something about her that I can't quite put my finger on. Something about her holds me captive, tempts me, demands that I sit up and pay fucking attention.

I reach out, my hand on her arm, and pull her backwards. Her body turns so we stand face to face, bodies inches apart, and fuck ... I'm pissed.

Pissed that she hates me. Pissed that she wants me. Frustrated that I want to just walk away but for some fucking reason I can't.

I was seduced by her kiss and moved by her with her boys yesterday. We basically fucked on the dance floor an hour ago and then she was with Surfer Joe and I swore it was a show. Something to play me like the games so many women use to get my attention. But then when I gave it to her, she left me high and dry without a chance to make the decision her eyes dared me to.

Choose her, pick her, drown in her.

She may not be playing the bullshit games, but it's still her fault. I use the need for her I don't want to feel to feed my anger. I don't want this—complications and estrogen fueled bullshit. I want a quick fuck, that's it. A roll in the sheets to satisfy the craving she's created and move on. I hold onto that lie and give the one reaction I can since the only other option my mind can think of is her beneath me.

And fucking hell, I want that.

"What the fuck do you think you're doing?" My voice is low and spiteful, my hand squeezing tighter on her arm to prevent it from sliding down her side. I yank her against me.

"Excuse me?"

She seems shocked that I'm angry. If I wasn't intimately familiar with the bite to her tongue, her reaction would leave me thinking she's used to being handled with kid gloves. But I know better than that, know she can hold her own.

"You have an annoying little habit of running away from me, Rylee." I watch the shock flicker across her face. Does she not see it? Kisses me and then runs at the benefit. Kisses me and runs at The House. Kisses me until I want so much more than just the small sample I had at the beach. That's a whole lot of tempt and not a lot of take on my part.

It's called blue balls, sweetheart. Something's got to give soon and I sure as fuck hope it's both our zippers.

"What's it to you, Mr. I-Send-Mixed-Signals?" She jerks her arm from my hand. Physical connection broken but fuck if the sexual tension isn't eating us alive.

"You're one to talk, *sweetheart*. Is that guy—is he what you really want, *Rylee*?" My mind flashes back to the fucker's hand on her, body up against hers. I see red then green. Fuck. The red I'm used to, but the jealousy is a whole different ball game I've never even taken a practice swing in. "A quick romp with Surfer Joe? You want to fuck him instead of *me*?"

I clench my jaw to control my need to taste those sexy-as-sin lips of hers she's scowling at me with. I fist my hands, that deep V of her dress calling to my fingers to dip inside and cup those tits she's pushing in my face as her chest heaves up and down from her angered breaths.

I deserve a goddamn medal for fighting this urge. For not touching when every ounce of me screams at me to plunder and pillage that mouth until it's swollen from use. My desire turns to anger because what I see in her eyes, what it makes me feel, isn't something I'm supposed to feel.

Fuck this.

Fuck her.

And fuck me because that's exactly the problem—wanting to fuck her—but newsflash, I know this is too goddamn complicated. A quick fuck is not supposed to be like this. Step away. Back the fuck off and go, Donavan. Turn around and walk the other way because those eyes of hers tell you this is going to be anything but simple.

I take a step closer.

Goddamn woman has me on an invisible line. Like she's cranking the reel and tightening the hook in my mouth before I even have a chance to taste the fucking bait.

We glare at each other, eyes devouring and warning all at the same time.

See? Complicated. Walk the fuck away. Save yourself.

"Isn't that what you want from me, Colton? A quick fuck to boost that fragile ego of yours? It seems you spend an awful lot of time trying to placate that weakness of yours. Besides, why do you care what I do? If I recall correctly, you were pretty occupied with the blonde on your arm."

I ignore the insult she hurls at me because I'm so focused on the tease of her body so tantalizingly close to mine. Tease me and insult me all at once. Contradictions like this are not supposed to be sexy. They are a downright mindfuck that I've learned to keep at restraining order distance. So why the hell do I still want her so fucking bad I can taste it?

I push away the ache to take her right now because she's right. I do just want a quick fuck.

Nice try, Donavan. Keep telling yourself that.

Maybe if I prove to her the asshole that I am, she'll take the reins here and walk the fuck away. Deny me what I want since I'm being such a pussy I can't do it myself and ironically am only thinking with my dick. Game plan in place, time to shift it in gear.

"*Raquel? She's inconsequential.*"

And I mean to sound like a chauvinistic asshole, that I think women are mere blips on my fucking radar, but there's something about *that word*—inconsequential—that is so fitting all of a sudden. It perfectly describes how Rylee made me feel when Raquel was at my side and she, herself, was standing in front of me.

Becks nailed it on the head the other night when I ditched sex with Raquel on the way home from the gala and he never even knew it.

"*Inconsequential?*" she says, eyes wide and irritation in her voice.

Good. She got the hint. Run baby, run. Let me get a good show as you walk away.

"Is that what I'd be to you after you fuck me? *Inconsequential?*"

Never.

Her words are a verbal backhand. Because as much as I want her to hate me and do what I can to spare me the complications I know she'd bring, when she throws herself in the same category as Raquel, the only word that flickers through my head is *never*.

Fucking hell, Donavan. If I keep this whiplash up—wanting her but not wanting her—I'm going to need to start wearing my HANS device outside of the goddamn car. I just wish I knew what it is about this woman that tells me she's not like the others. And not just because she's kept her legs closed when most others would have theirs spread by now.

Fuck if I know, but I'm done with this game. She just threw out a challenge she didn't even realize when she dared me to prove her different than Raquel.

I want. And I need. And hell if I'm not going to taste her again, fuck her mouth with my tongue to try and show her how badly I want to do the same elsewhere.

Prove to her how she could never be inconsequential even though that's all I really want her to be. The only thing I can allow when the cards fall where they may.

I take a step closer. Her back bumps against the wall, and I lift my hand toward her face but then pull it back.

Somehow I have a conscience and it's just decided to show the hell up. Because this is perfect fucking timing to tell me I can't do this to her, fuck with her to fix me. Like I didn't know already that it's not fair to her, something she doesn't deserve.

Sex without strings is something I've always done so why am I thinking this now? Why didn't I think it earlier when I ditched the Merit execs? I'm not a good guy so why, when all I want is to slide between her thighs and lose myself for a bit, do I suddenly feel like I need to warn her in yet another way?

I stare at her, try to convey my thoughts and hope she gets them.

Run! I want scream at her. Tell her to take the fuck off down the hall and not look back. Explain that I'm a selfish bastard who takes what he wants without worries about collateral damage because I have a feeling that once I have her I'm going to need to destroy some things to prevent me from wanting her again.

Ease the ache. Bury the pain. Fuck her over in the end because she'll hope there's more when I can only give her less.

Can you handle me, Rylee? You fix the broken but there's no hope left here. Can you live with that? Can you handle temporary when your eyes say you're a forever? Do you want me? Can you live with sex and secrets and a selfish son of a bitch who will use you in the end?

Tell me no. Please tell me no because I can't find it in myself to walk the fuck away like I should. Make the choice for me. Push me away. Hurt me.

She holds my gaze and then lifts her chin in a subtle nod.

Fuck! Every part of my body screams the word, each one holding a different meaning to the reaction.

She just said yes, and I swallow the fact that my warnings were all in my head. My excuse to fall back and ease my guilt later when I walk away.

But right now? Right now, I'm taking what she's offering. Restraint obliterated and my dick in command.

Add another demon to the pile within because I sure as fuck don't deserve a quick stop in Heaven before I take the long ride to Hell, but I'm taking it.

Without thought, my hands frame her face and my lips are on hers. I'm hungry for the taste of her, desperate for the feel of her. Smooth skin, gentle moans, soft against hard.

She's like a fix to an addiction. I thought if I had a taste, I'd want it less, but fuck me, all I can think of is more. Take more, want more, feel more, need more.

One hand is on her neck, the other on her back, and I pull her against me, need her against me from chest to knee. My mouth takes, nips, and sips. Her reactions spur me on. The moan in her throat when I suck on her tongue. The arch of her back when I tug on her lip with my teeth. Her body begs for the things her lips refuse to ask me for. And fuck if it's not the hottest thing to know she wants this as desperately as I do, but I need to be in control here. Need to own the situation and the shit I keep pushing out of my head.

Her hands fist my shirt, need burning a hole through me, my dick aching, my body waiting to claim. In reflex, I grab her hands and pin them above the wall over our heads so she's completely open to me.

Mine to control. To set the pace. To prevent her from revealing the shit that needs to stay behind lock and key.

I bring my free hand down to hold her chin so I can brand her lips again. Kiss her senseless so she has no other fucking option than to say yes to the question I so desperately want to ask. But when my fingers hold her there, her eyes flutter up to look into mine, dark lashes framing the most unique of colors. And although my dick is rock hard and wanting to act, I stumble over thoughts I don't mean to say but that fall out of my mouth before I can stop them.

"*Not inconsequential*, Rylee. You could never be inconsequential." I close my eyes and rest my forehead against hers to give myself a moment to try and figure out what the fuck is wrong with me. "No—you and me—together, that would make you *mine. Mine.*"

My confession shocks me. I mean it's one thing to think the words and another fucking thing to say them. Hell yes, they're true, but since when do I say crap like this? Give a woman a drawer for her shit when I only plan on letting her pass through the ever-revolving bedroom door.

My honesty scares the shit out of me. Makes me question when I never second guess myself.

I take a deep breath and step back, releasing her hands still held by mine, our eyes never breaking. And I don't know what it is now that I'm asking her because hell if I know. I'm confused as fuck, desperate to bury myself in her and at the same time trying to figure out what this feeling in the pit of my stomach is.

It's always been pleasure to bury the pain. The sex to quiet my head, override the shame coating my soul, so why the hell is my head screaming right now?

She reaches out to me, her fingers scraping against my abdomen, and fuck if my body doesn't jolt at the connection. I cuffed her hands because I'm used to being in control, used to setting the pace, so why the fuck am I not stopping her. Why do her fingers feel like she's lighting my skin on fire? Like she's burning me with her touch.

I close my eyes, her hands on my back, and my breath labored with the desire that's so strong I feel like I'm ready to snap. To take without asking.

And then her lips touch mine. Soft and sweet. That fucking perfect contradiction against her hands pulling my body into hers. Her tongue teases by tracing my bottom lip and thoughts of how it can trace the line of my cock have me reaching up to touch her face.

I make my hands go there so I can control the need to rip zippers and feast on her flesh, take the usual route when she is anything but my usual, when the situation is so far from my norm that I'm flying solo without a pit crew for back-up. So instead I force myself to part her lips with my tongue, challenge myself to see how long I can last with this tender and soft when all I really want to do is be rough and sate my greed.

I push my limits. Control the desperation. Even when her fingers dig in my shoulders and urge me on, I rein it in. Every time she moves, my dick rubs against her lower belly and I kiss her a little deeper to lose myself for just a moment. To encourage my resistance.

And then she sighs.

Sweet Christ. How can such a simple sound make a man want to lose his fucking control when he's already held out against every other form of her unbeknownst seduction? But that sigh … fuck, the sound owns me in ways I never thought possible.

I can't take the assault on my senses anymore. I just fucking can't. I press my hands on the wall on either side of her head, my last attempt at restraint. And I'm such a dumbass that I think if my hands are not on her, I can control my urge to take her as I see fit. Take her in ways I don't think by the innocence in her eyes she's experienced yet.

Because shit, she's a soft and slow, make love not just fuck kind of girl and I'm the exact opposite. Physical overriding emotional every day because I can't do emotional. And she deserves so much better than me. I might be a selfish prick but I know this much.

The problem is she's so goddamn addictive that even though I've occupied my hands, I allow myself one small hit. I rest my forehead against the curve of her neck, nose buried. My chest heaves for air. The scent of her perfume and shampoo make my balls tighten and use up my last ounce of control.

"Sweet Jesus, Rylee." I lace kisses along her shoulder while my body aches painfully to have her wrapped around me. "We need to get out of here before you unman me in the hallway."

I raise my head and look into her eyes. Last chance, Ryles. Escape while you can. But she stands her ground, unwavering, accepting of the warning in my eyes and the dominance in my stance.

"Come." God help me because when all is said and done, I think I'm going to need it to walk away from her. She bites her bottom lip to stop it from quivering. Even she knows I'm inviting her into the lion's den.

I give her a soft smile, pretending I can't see the vulnerability in her eyes, ignoring it as I draw her further in … and that makes me even worse of a man than I already thought.

We walk, desire leading us and desperation owning our thoughts. I think I mumble an explanation that I have a room, but I'm not sure because my thoughts are consumed by every single thing about her. Fucking consumed when I've never been this way before.

I usher her into the elevator, unlock the penthouse all the while my dick is begging me to push the red button, halt the elevator right here, right now and take her on the floor. Feed the greed and be done with her.

Return to familiar ground and be the asshole I know that I am.

I reach out to touch her back, begin the process, but I can't bring myself to do it. I can't treat her like she's inconsequential and prove her right. I mutter something about her hair, asking why she's changed the curls I've thought about holding in one hand so I can watch while my cock fucks her mouth. She responds about not fitting a mold but shit my mind is back onto the image of her bobbing her head up and down with hollowed out cheeks and I can't focus.

"Sometimes change is good." She's staring at me when I break from my thoughts.

I mumble a response about liking her curls, sounding so innocent but really being anything but because my mind is thinking about how fucking bad I want her right now. And then her comment breaks into my thoughts … *sometimes change is good.*

Is that what this is? A change from my typical so it's got my dick in a twist?

Gotta be.

The warnings flood my head again. I need to tell her I'm in uncharted territory, that I'm not sure what the hell is going on, but the one thing I do know for certain is that she deserves a chance to leave before I can't turn back.

"You have one chance to walk away." The elevator dings, shattering my concentration that's scattered as it is. I stare at her, need to see her eyes and hear her tell me she wants this without hesitation. "I won't be able to walk away, Rylee."

And that's exactly what I need to do to ease the unsettling I already feel deep down in the parts of me I buried so very long ago. In the dark recesses where the promises I made to myself feel like they are beginning to unseat themselves.

Am I doing the right thing here when I know that fucking her just might hurt ... both her and me?

Fuck. That's exactly what all this is. I turn from her, needing a minute myself to decide whether the discorded peace in my soul is worth disturbing.

Snap out of it, Donavan. Quit being such a pussy. You have a woman willing right now. The same one you've passed up Raquel and her blow job skills for twice. You obviously want this. So fucking take it. You know how to walk when the sex turns to emotion so get your shoes and put them by the door for an easy escape.

But fucking hell take what she's offering. Man the fuck up. Tell her how it's going to be and then do it. Give her the option to only say yes because sweet fucking Jesus, if her kiss is that goddamn sweet imagine what the fuck her pussy tastes like.

Problem solved. Everything back on its mental shelf.

I stab the button with my finger for the elevator door and then hang my head as I figure out how to say it all. "I want to take my time with you, Rylee. I want to build you up nice and slow and sweet like you need. Push you to crash over that edge. And then I want to fuck you the way I need to. Fast and hard until you're screaming my name. The way I've wanted to since you fell out of that storage closet and into my life. Once we leave this elevator, I don't think I'll have enough control to stop ... to pull away from you, Rylee. I. Can't. Resist. You."

My confession is cathartic. Allows me to fuck her without the guilt because I'm giving her a choice. More steady in my shoes that I momentarily stepped out of, I finally turn back to face her. I need to see her eyes when I give her the only choice I'm going to until after we've come and are panting out of breath and spent.

"Decide, Rylee. *Yes. Or. No.*"

Driven

Chapter Fourteen

The night after. Rylee and Colton finally have sex and then he gets out of the bed like she burned him, made it apparent he's made a huge mistake sleeping with her. Rylee gathers her dignity and pride, throws the caution flag up, and walks out.

She has a restless night filled with nightmares from her past. She and Haddie have a *come-to-Colton* talk about how it's okay to have mindless sex with him to get over Max, about how it's okay to clear the cobwebs and live a little.

Rylee wakes up with a new resolve from the tearful woman who left the hotel the night before. She's going to try to just go with the flow when it comes to Colton. See what happens. She goes for a run and when she returns, guess who's standing in her driveway waiting for the woman who ran out on him?

There was something humorous in figuring out Colton's reaction to Rylee's transformation from the upset woman the night before to this confident temptress challenging him with her words and her body. It was also a hard scene to write because once again, Colton's motivations were almost schizophrenic in nature. His continual need to explain to himself why he's there, that he's just trying to be a good guy, apologize for being an ass, makes you want to shake him so he sees what's right in front of him.

WHY THE FUCK AM I here? Seriously, Donavan? Chasing her like a damn chick after last night. After I fucked her and then freaked the hell out and basically pushed her away. Like that doesn't have *douche-bag* written all over it.

Walk away, Donavan. Lift the right foot, then the left, and walk around the fucking Rover. Leave the complication alone and ease what-the-fuck-ever is that weird pressure in my chest.

Do it.

Now.

Move your ass.

I look up, conviction in my head but resistance in my soul, and the air punches from my lungs. Lead now weighing down my fucking flip-flopped feet.

My God she's gorgeous. Like knock me to my knees gorgeous. What girl can be sweaty in workout gear, jeans and a T-shirt, or dressed to the hilt like last night and be hot as fuck in all three?

She runs the rest of the way toward me and hell yes I look at the way her tits bounce in her snug little tank thingy. I groan inwardly as I remember the weight of them in my hands. The taste of them on my tongue.

"Hi." She breathes out and although she looks winded I like to think her quickened breath is because of me.

"Hello, Rylee." It's all I can manage to say. Thoughts flicker through my head. How I should apologize. How I should demand to know why she makes me feel like this when I don't even know what *this* is.

"What are you doing here?" Confusion mars her gorgeous face as those eyes of hers search mine for an explanation I can't even give her. One that I know but am not able to put sound to the words because then it would make her ... make this too fucking real.

And I don't do real. I do quick. I do easy. I do rules and draw lines that never get crossed.

So why the fuck am I here, then?

I look at her, such a goddamn contradiction in everything she is, and have the urge to tell her the truth but know the truth will push her away. I want to tell her she burned me last night. Fucked me into feeling more than just the physical when I'm so used to being numb. Made me feel raw and vulnerable when I'm always guarded.

And I couldn't handle it. She looked in my eyes so deeply I could see the truths she saw there reflected in her own eyes and it scared the fuck out of me.

Demons best be left untouched or else they destroy. Collateral damage be damned. Been there, done that shit.

She angles her head at me. Her eyes still reflect hurt, but I also see surprise and thank fuck for that because it means I still have a shot. The question is after last night and the goddamn hurricane of emotions that ripped through me during and after we had sex, I'm not quite sure what *the shot* I'm looking for is.

Redemption? Apology? Forgiveness? Another chance?

Pick one, Donavan, because she proved last night she doesn't play the games you're used to so figure out the answer to her question, the one you don't even know the answer to yourself.

"Well, according to you, I took the checkered flag last night, Rylee …" I say as I take a step toward her trying to snap my thoughts in line, make up a reason for being here besides the need to make sure she's okay when I could have just picked up the fucking phone. I resist the urge to reach out and touch her because I know if I do, my dick will rise to the occasion and do the talking for me. And fuck if I know what it will say.

She licks her lips, dick beginning to win the internal thought process, when I suddenly figure out my angle … my in … my stupid-ass excuse for showing up the morning after like some pussy-whipped douchebag. Because Christ, you can't get pussy whipped after just one taste. Shit like that takes time to acquire.

Or so I've heard.

This man might be drawn to the pussy palace but fuck if its queen will hand out orders that I'll obey.

I take another step toward her, still undecided about my excuse for being here when I glance down momentarily and see her nipples harden through her tank. That's always a plus. At least I know she's still attracted to me. Let's see if I can make her like me again. Give me another chance.

Bingo. Truth shall set me free. There's the answer. I just want another chance when I've never wanted one before.

And therein lies the second question, another chance at what though?

I shake the thought, her eyes asking me to finish the question I left hanging. "… but I seem to have neglected to collect my trophy."

"*Trophy?*"

Hmm. Maybe not such a good idea, now that I think about it. Fix this, Donavan. Fix how you just compared her to something that sits on the shelf and collects dust.

Play, player, play.

"Yes. You." I reach for her hand and pull her into me. Her breath hitches: *check*. Her heart's pounding: *check*.

I've still got my game despite feeling like she knocked it off its field last night. Thank fuck for that.

And then she looks up at me and that damn defiance is back, and I know we're about to go a round. She might be affected but fuck if she's going to back down. Let's see if this gets us where we need to be.

Bring it on, baby.

"Well, Ace, I think you've got your eyes on the wrong prize." She pushes against my chest and steps back, a smirk on her face. "If all you're looking for is a trophy, you have your bevy of beauties you can pick from. I'm sure that one of them would be more than willing to be a *trophy* on your arm." She steps past me and when she turns around, our eyes meet and she holds her ground. "You could probably start by calling Raquel, is it? I'm sure she'll forgive you for last night. I mean, you were … *decent*. She's probably thrilled with *decent*."

Knee-jerk reaction has me grabbing her arm and spinning her around when she goes to walk away again.

Decent? *Decent*? You want to play dirty, huh? I have a whole chest full of toys we can use if you want to go that route, but first things first.

"*Decent*, huh?" I step in closer to her, wanting so bad to taste the defiance on her lips but refraining. I came here today expecting to find her hurt and all I'm getting is obstinance. I'm confused how the woman who left me last night with tears in her eyes is the same fucking one that stands before me. What has happened in the last ten hours? Shit, I came here to apologize, salvage the chance to have her again so I can figure out what the fuck kind of hold she has over me. Try to see what it is about her that has me coming back for seconds when I prefer my meals to be more varied because shit, if you keep on moving, keep on sampling, no one can get too close.

I'm trying to figure this all out and then she goes and calls my abilities on the carpet when we both know last night was anything but decent. Hell, she blew the doors off the damn bedroom and chiseled away at everything I guard. She wants to pretend I was decent, that she wasn't affected? Go right ahead because I know avoidance when I see it and fuck if she's not using this newfound confidence to cover something up. The question is what?

And that in itself is comical since I'm the king of avoidance.

Interesting.

She stares at me as I try to make sense of this new set of unspoken rules. Her eyes flicker with amusement, her words still hanging in the air between us, still taunting me, still tempting me.

And fuck it. I'm all in. Play me, Ryles, because I'm just getting warmed up. The two of us can pretend we're whole, void of baggage, and see how far that gets us. Objective just went from getting another *chance* at who the fuck knows what to working that sweet spot between her thighs again so she has no option but to admit she's wrong. Admit that her description of decent would be fan-fucking-orgasmic if she were speaking about any other man's skills. And then even though I don't want to care, don't want to fuck with another person's demons, I'm going to figure out what the hell she's hiding.

Decent walks away and doesn't care. Decent gets themselves off without thinking of the other person's needs. Fucking decent, my ass.

She bites her bottom lip deliberately and flutters her lashes like she's innocent. Damn tease. "Hmm, a smidgen above average, I'd say."

I step into her, my mouth close, our chests touching, and just stay there. Taunting her with anticipation until I hear her exhale the breath she's holding. "Maybe I need to show you again. I assure you that *decent* is not an accurate assessment."

She pushes against my chest again because it appears she can't handle the heat. She can talk the talk but she sure as fuck can't walk the walk. Then again, the way she's strutting her ass toward the door right now makes me take the statement back.

Fuck. I know how those curves feel beneath my hands, riding my cock, milking my orgasm. We were so fucking far from decent it's not even funny.

"I need to go stretch. Are you gonna come?"

Sweet Jesus. Seriously? "If you keep moving your ass like that, I am," I mutter under my breath, feet following without a second thought.

I follow her into the house, eyes scanning the interior. Clean, classic, just like I'd expect from her. I sit on the couch wondering where our little charade is going to lead us now. I spot a few possible surfaces that I can more than prove my point on.

But my attention and thoughts are pulled to Ry as she settles on the floor in front of me and proceeds to spread her legs as wide as they go before leaning forward and pressing her chest to the floor. My dick hardens immediately at the sight of her, her impressive flexibility, and the memory of the tight, wet pussy sitting within that V of her thighs.

Shit, she's fighting dirty trying to jog my memory of how she fucks like a sinner and feels like Heaven, as if it wasn't permanently scored into me.

So why am I looking at her eyes and not her tits? Why am I anticipating the next round of verbal sparring when I should be using smooth lines to lure her back so I can prove her wrong?

"So, Colton," she says, breaking through my civil war of thoughts and my absolute focus on her proffered tits and stupendous ass. "What can I do for you?"

Shit, we can start with you on your knees, me on the couch, and your mouth on my cock. The immediate image makes my head spin with need.

"Christ, Rylee!" I bark the words out, trying to stop her stretching, stop my thinking, when I'm the one that's supposed to be taking control of this conversation so I can prove my point in more ways than one. And hell if every ounce of testosterone in my body says "*please don't stop.*" Fuck getting the upper hand in the argument because when all is said and done, all that matters is that I get to bury myself in her regardless of how the point is made.

"What?" She bats her eyelashes again. Innocent façade front and center.

"We need to talk about last night." I change the subject. Need to think of rainbows and unicorns and shit to calm my dick the fuck down. Allow me to give my apology for last night. Set one wrong to right before diving right into the next with her because deep down I know we are one of those disasters waiting to happen. Beautiful and devastating all at the same time.

The quick fuck I wanted to ease the ache for her turned out to be so much more than that. It's moved into uncharted territory for me, and no matter which way I look at this, she's added a complication to my simple, fuck-more-care-less lifestyle. She's made me want her more than once, made me pursue when I don't chase, and has me here apologizing when I'm a take-me-as-I-am-or-get-the-hell-out kind of guy.

But fuckin' A, if complicated is flexible like that, I'll take it.

And there she goes again. Making me lose my train of fucking thought as she lies on her back, pulls one leg up, and lifts her head to look at me over the mound of her pussy.

She thinks she can just sit and stretch and she's going to win this little unspoken war we have going? That I'm just going to kowtow because it looks like she can wrap her feet behind her head and makes me think of the positions I can put that body in? That I'd give up the battle of wills here over something that clearly was mind-blowing?

It's time I get some answers myself because if we're both warming up on the same field, then fuck if I'm not ready to go one-on-one with her. I admit that I'm an asshole for treating her like shit last night because I couldn't handle that weird fucking pressure in my chest, but what does that make her? Leave with tears but now flirt with me like she's up for another go?

Goddamn women.

Too compli-fucking-cated is what they are. But if I'm going to test the waters again, I need to get my head wrapped around what's in hers so I can get us back on the sex-without-a-future plan, then I need to know what she's thinking. "Why'd you leave? Why'd you run away? *Again*."

She switches legs and moans in pleasure, followed by my name. "Colton—"

Just like she fucking did last night.

"Can you please stop?" I can't help it but if she keeps this shit up I'm gonna come in my pants like a goddamn teenager. And there she goes again, rolling over so her ass is in my face. Thoughts of taking her from behind fill my head: hands gripping her hips, dick bottoming out as my pelvis slaps against her ass. "Christ! You in those yoga pants all limber and bending in half—you're making me lose my concentration here."

And something else if you keep it up.

Those violet eyes taunt me as they look over her shoulder. "Hmm?"

Oh, sweetheart, you know exactly what you're doing. And so do I. You can't beat this player at his own game.

"You're gonna make me forget my apologies and take you right here on the floor. Hard and fast, Rylee."

"Oh!" It's all she can say, and I feel a slight thrill of victory for knocking her off stride. But fuck if her lips formed in that little O shape don't have my thoughts drifting back to my couch blowjob fantasy from moments before. "Although I'm sure it's me who should be apologizing, Colton."

And there she goes, fucking up my thoughts of how I don't want to feel anything for her by taking the blame for last night. The selfless saint martyring for the selfish sinner.

I'm starting to get irritated. Don't make me feel. Don't make me think of things outside what I can give you. I'm here trying to be bigger than the man I usually am by making sure she's all right. That's it. Simple and uncomplicated. And she says something like that and knocks me back. Makes me feel like she did last night when I shoved up out of the bed and left her naked body I would have rather lost myself in, long into the early hours of the morning. But no, I can't allow anyone to get close to me and fuck if she's not bringing us right back there with her attempt to apologize.

"Why'd you leave, Rylee?"

The harshness in my tone causes her to stare at me a moment

before she answers. "A number of reasons, Colton. I told you, I'm just not *that* kind of girl. I don't do one-night stands."

"Who said it was a one-night stand?" I throw her own excuse for leaving back at her and immediately question myself and the implication I've now left open for interpretation. That's exactly what I need with her to avoid the shit she unknowingly brought to life last night. What the fuck am I doing here besides muddying up the fucking complicated water even more?

"What?" Confusion flickers over her face. "You lost me. I thought commitment wasn't your thing."

I lost me too, sweetheart.

"It isn't." I shrug. Time to turn the subject back to you. Make you explain because fuck if I'm going to delve into my closet of nightmares to explain myself. "I don't believe you."

"*What?*" She's confused. Good, because that makes two of us. Thank fuck, though, I'm the one with the reins now.

"Your excuse for running last night. I don't buy it. Why'd you leave, Rylee?" Give me a real reason. Tell me you got spooked the fuck out too. That it just wasn't me. Tell me you hate me. That you want me. Tell me anything to ease the fucking schizophrenic thoughts owning my head right now because you've turned this man who never needs anything to one who needed to see you. And fuck if I can figure out why.

I need to get this—us—back to where I'm comfortable. A good time with no future.

"I just—" She sighs, fiddling with her ponytail thing, and I can now see her nerves. Can sense her unease. And when she meets my eyes again, she knocks the gas from my tank because they are so full of conflicting emotion. "You made it clear that you were done with me. With us, cursing adamantly to demonstrate why my presence was no longer needed."

No longer needed? That's what she thought? "Sweet Jesus, Rylee!" Why is it with any other woman I'd be ecstatic that she thought that. Would make it easier to have the talk with her that I need to have and lay down the law about the only things I can give her, but hearing the words from Rylee causes a tightness in my chest.

She thought I was done with her. Leave it be, Donavan. Shut your fucking mouth and leave. Apologize for being an ass and walk away.

"Do you have any idea … you made me … I just want to protect you from—" I can't even finish my thought my head's such a mess. *Yeah, the get up and leave idea worked real well there. Fuck me.* I shove up out of the chair and head toward the window, toward an escape.

How do I explain that the way she made me feel caused the demons I'd buried deep down to start to whisper that I don't deserve anything from her? That I saw myself using her—hurting her—like those before her and for the first time ever, I couldn't do it. Knew she didn't deserve it.

Shit just got real—fast. Real when all I want is to go back to our bantering foreplay. I need to get this back on ground I can walk on because right now I'm starting to freak the fuck out.

"I asked you to stay. That's all I can give you right now, Rylee. All I'm good for." I know I sound like an asshole, know that she just said I hurt her and my response was anything but an apology, but at the same time she doesn't have a fucking clue how normally I'd say "my way or the highway" and instead I'm trying to explain a bit of myself when I never have before.

"C'mon, Colton, we both know you didn't mean it. Let's just say I left last night for reasons you don't want to know about," she finally says, eyes lifting to meet mine, and fuck if I can tell what they are trying to say to me that her words aren't. I wonder if these reasons are the cause of her sudden change in demeanor from last night to this morning. "I've got lots of excess baggage, Ace."

A part of me sighs in relief at *the out* she's giving me without another word. The funny thing is that even though my feet itch to walk, I can't bring myself to move because my head has other thoughts.

"Oh, Rylee, I know all about baggage, sweetheart. I have enough of it to fill up a 747 and then some." I say the words without thinking. My immediate instinct is to jump back when I realize the little bit of myself I just gave her. That I'm the pilot of a plane so weighed down with fucking baggage that I might crash at any time. It's not fucking much, but it's a shitload of a confession for me.

I see the shock flicker through her eyes followed by the curiosity. How that comment doesn't scare the hell out of her, I have no clue. She's fearless and I love it. Love that we're standing here in this goddamn minefield of shit and yet she continues to hold my gaze and tempt me, dare me, when the minute the words clear my mouth most would run the other way without so much as a see-ya.

Of course with the exception of those that want something out of being with me. And the way she keeps fighting me, I sure as fuck know she falls into the one percent that doesn't.

"This could be interesting," I say, taking a step toward her, my eyes scraping over her curves and my mind trying to find my footing in this foreign fucking territory. How is it I want to keep this on my terms—keep her at arms' length—and yet at the same time want to figure out why I felt how I felt last night, how I feel right now?

Want my cake and eat her too.

The thought staggers me, fucks with my head, because I don't know how that's going to be possible when all I've thought about since she left the hotel last night was seeing her again. So I do what I came here for, the one thing I know that will settle the war of shit inside of me, quiet my head for just a second, so I can think this through. I reach out to touch her.

I tug her hair out of the bun and fist my hands in the curls as they fall. Her eyes shock open as I pull her head back and parted lips distract my thoughts as I'd hoped.

And just when I'm about to break our stare because she's looking at me again in that way that says she sees more than I intend to give her, she throws out a challenge to my comment.

"How so?" Her voice may be soft, might even reflect a hint of nerves, but she's still asking.

"Well, it seems that your baggage makes you so scared to feel you constantly pull away. Run from me." I trace my finger down her bare arm, the need to touch her consuming me like an addiction. "Whereas mine? My baggage? It makes me crave the sensory over-load of physicality—the stimulating indulgence of skin on skin. Of you beneath me."

I mean it as a kind of warning, a simple you're going to fall for me while I just want to fuck you. What a woman wants versus what a man wants. Simple, uncomplicated, right up until she sighs that soft sigh she did last night when I pushed into her for the first time and fuck if I can hold back any longer. I lean in and kiss her, tell myself to slow the fuck down when all I want to do is own her lips.

Her lips, Donavan, not her heart, because I'm trying to keep this on my simple terms.

Because that's *all* I want.

And fuck if I've not kissed a woman like this before—slow and relentless—but something happens with Rylee. Each taste, every sound I coax that hums in her throat begins to seep into parts of me that have been dead for so long. I deepen the kiss. I have no intention of doing this, feeling this way, and I'm sure if my lips weren't drugged by her taste, I'd be pulling away, wanting the end game and not enjoy the fucking journey to get there.

But when she slides her hands up my torso, skin to skin, something happens. It's like the whip of desire snaps and imprints everything about her inside of me.

Fuckin' A was I wrong. Touch her, kiss her to quiet my head? More like set it on fucking fire with thoughts of possibilities I don't want and lust I need to sate. That flutter of panic I had last night flashes through me as I pull back from her lips, needing a minute to settle the shit I don't want to feel but is back with a fucking vengeance.

I pull her into my chest and wrap my arms around her so she can't look into my eyes and see the shit I don't even understand. And I'm trying to process it all, trying to tell myself it's a fucking fluke that it happened again, just the need to fuck her again, that's all. I'm so wrapped up in my thoughts the words are out of my mouth before I can filter them. "It's unfathomable how much I want you, Rylee. How much I'm drawn to you."

An unexpected confession for both her and for me.

"Rylee ..." I'm flustered and I never get flustered. Fuck! I need some time to figure this all out. My reaction to last night, to right now, to how she fits so fucking perfect in my arms. Man, I'm all for turning over a new leaf, trying new shit out, but this is more like shaking the goddamn tree bare.

Breathe, Donavan. Fucking Breathe.

I close my eyes and then she makes a hmm sound as she nuzzles under my neck and I say, "Go out with me—on a real date. Go out with me, not because I paid for a date with you but because you want to. Say yes, Ryles. It's unimaginable how much I want you to say yes."

Where the fuck did that come from, Donavan? I'm freaking the fuck out and want to put it back where I'm comfortable, have a talk to mitigate her expectations of where this can and can't go, but I go and say something like that? How am I ever going be able to fix this now, rein it in before she starts getting too close and I start doing what I do best—shove her away?

She leans back, like she's as shocked as I am from my words, and looks at me. And for some reason I don't break our gaze and let her see just a glimpse of the riot inside of me before I glance away. But she pulls me back to her when she runs a hand against my cheek and then steps on her toes and presses a kiss to my lips.

"Yes," she whispers.

I nod my head at her and pull her back into my chest. "Tonight?"

Rylee, what the fuck are you doing to me?

She falls silent and a part of me freezes while the other part hopes she says yes. I can't give her too much time to think about the shit she's seen in my eyes and the baggage I told her about. She's a smart girl, she'll figure out I'm bad fucking news, a heartbreak waiting to happen, and head for the fucking hills.

And the thought scares the shit out of me. I keep telling myself once I talk with her, I'll set things straight and she'll fall in line like all of the other arrangements I've had. There will be nothing more between us but great sex, a date for an event, and a kick-ass charity partnership. But if that's all I want, why am I here? Why do I care if she says yes or no to another date?

Why do I want her like no fucking tomorrow?

"I'll be here at six to pick you up, Rylee." Time to find out. Test the waters and then jump ship.

Or walk the plank.

She looks back up at me, her bottom lip between her teeth, and hell if I know what I'm doing but fuck if I'm not going to have a good time trying to figure it out.

I lift my thumb and rub it over her bottom lip. "See you then, sweetheart." I walk to the front door as she says goodbye, my dick begging for those lips and my head hoping to make sense of the door I just turned the key in that I have no business unlocking.

I stop and turn to look at her one last time. "Hey, Ryles? No more running away from me."

I flash her a quick grin before I leave and I wonder who I'm talking to about not running away, her or me.

Driven

Chapter Twenty-One

One of my favorite scenes in DRIVEN, the bad boy standing up for the bullied Aiden. We see a bit of the broken man standing up for the damaged little boy he once was by helping. A small victory of sorts.

Then we follow them to the coffee shop and see the moment Colton decides that maybe he should let Rylee in a bit, see where it takes them, and changes the direction of the entire story. Almost a new starting point if you will ...

I REV THE ASTON. HER purr reverberates against the concrete walls in front of me and echoes through the early morning over the collective chatter that fills the air. If the boys only knew how many times as a kid I dealt with this shit. Fucking know-it-all punks who picked on me because I was that *"pity-case"* the Westins took in—what most assumed was an attempt to keep their holier than thou public persona up.

Yeah right. If those fuckers only knew the hell my parents had saved me from. A bully's fists and words were nothing compared to what I'd already lived through.

Sticks and stones. Sticks and stones.

Even if I didn't look in the rearview mirror at the boys and their grins in the backseat, I'd know they were smiling from the unmistakable energy zinging in the car. They'll get their due. I'll make sure of it.

I rev the car again, and I can see Ry tense beside me as she prevents herself from telling me I'm breaking the rules. Rule follower and rule breaker. Opposites must really fucking attract. Huh? If she only knew how opposite we really were.

God I would love to tear into this parking lot and lay some rubber. Give the boys a real entrance that would leave the rest of the students talking for months. It takes all of my restraint not to. Instead, I slide the Aston in between the curb and the waiting line of suburbanite moms in their SUVs or minivans and their judgmental attitudes.

Time to make an entrance, boys. Time to turn the tables, give them some positive attention for once, and put those fucking bullies to shame.

I park askew up onto the dip in the sidewalk, angling the car on purpose so that the boys can make their grand entrance. I rev the motor a few more times for good measure before opening my door and climbing out of the car. I take a quick look and notice a few of the moms in their sweatpants look my way. They stop, angling sunglasses down to see if I'm who they really think I am.

Damn straight, ladies. In the fucking flesh.

I stretch my arms above my head, taking my time and groaning aloud for good measure as I watch mouths fall lax and hands fly immediately to smooth down their unruly morning ponytails. I walk around the front of the car and stifle a laugh as I notice the shuffling through purses and sudden appearance of lipstick tubes. Fucking pretentious women.

Like I'd go for you when I have *her* in my front seat. Are you fucking kidding me? Plastic, botox, and ditz or real, intelligent, and sexy as fuck? A few weeks ago the decision may have been different, but now—since Rylee—there isn't one to be made.

Call me crazy.

Or pussy whipped.

I open the door for Rylee. My eyes instinctively scrape over her body and recall perfectly the feel of those curves beneath mine. She smirks at me—humor and curiosity mixed in her eyes—as she wonders how the reckless, quick to throw a punch Colton Donavan is going to handle these grade school punks.

I can't help the smile on my face as I squat down and flip the seat forward. The looks on Scooter, Aiden, and Ricky's faces are fucking priceless. I help them from the car and place my arms on their shoulders, the whisper of my name zipping through the crowd at my back.

That's right. *They're with me, folks.* No fucking with them any more.

I lean over to Aiden, the look of shock and fear and pride on his face makes me want to grab him and hug him. Tell him that no matter who you are or where you come from, there's always someone who'll stand up for you. "Do you see the bullies, buddy?"

His bruised little face looks around the crowd, and I know the minute he sees the punks. His body stiffens and fear or shame flickers momentarily through his eyes. For that look on his face alone, the fuckers should be suspended. I look to where he's staring and know instantly who my targets are. Seriously? I'm transported back twenty years in time and the fuckers could be interchangeable with those that tormented my years of school.

"Well, champ, it's time to go prove a point."

I urge the boys forward with my hands as I stand in the middle of the three of them, purposely moving as a solid unit. Mess with one of us, you get all of us. I can sense Ry's apprehension as to how I'm going to handle this, but she really needs to give me more fucking credit.

I plaster an easy going grin to my face as we approach the boys. Gonna kill them with fucking kindness. "Hey, guys!" I say in greeting as the boys' eyes widen like saucers and the shit-eating grins fade from their lips. "Hey, Aid, are these the boys that didn't believe you were my buddy?"

"Yeah," he croaks and looks up at me. And if I already didn't love this fucking kid, the look on his face makes me love him even more now. Eyes startled. Freckles scrunching. Lips turning up at the corners in a disbelieving smile. Yeah, *buddy*, you're more than worth sticking up for. It's time to start believing it.

"Oh man!" I say turning back to *dumb and dumber.* "You

should've seen Aiden on Sunday. I let him bring six of his friends, including Ricky and Scooter here..." I squeeze their shoulders to let them know they're just as worthy "...with him to the track to test out the car, and boy were they the biggest help to me! We had so much fun!"

I can feel all three boys stand a little taller and I know that a bit of confidence has been restored in their damaged souls. They've still got a long way to go, but it's a start.

"Too bad you guys aren't friends of his or maybe you could have gone too!" It takes everything I have to not tell *dumber* to close his mouth because he's going to catch a fly if he keeps looking at me like that. Then again, it serves him right for picking on the weak. No, not weak—after everything these kids have been through, definitely not weak. *More like damaged.* Yeah damaged but hopefully repairable.

Unlike me.

The school bell buzzes and it's only now I realize the crowd around us. I've been too busy restoring the boys' dignity to notice. And honestly, fuck if I care. I note the bystanders' eyes flicker over my shoulder, and I have a feeling the dipshit authority is near. I don't even have to check because I know the look he'll have on his face already. It's embedded in my memory from too many trips myself. I guess pissing off principals is one thing I'll never stop doing whether I'm thirteen or thirty.

It's time to make sure the crowd understands where I stand in regards to the boys. I ratchet my smile up a notch and wink at the bullies. "Bye, boys! Make sure you say 'hi' to my man Aiden here when you see him in class!"

They just continue to stare at me as The Suit uses his hands to physically guide them toward the front doors of the school. He then turns back to Aiden, Ricky, and Scooter. "Boys, you too," he says in a monotone that makes me think of the teacher in Ferris Bueller.

I glance over at Rylee for the first time during this whole display, and I can see her fighting back a smirk. She just subtly nods her head at me when I ask her with my eyes if this is the prick taking sides. It takes everything I have to keep my temper reined in this time because the boys are still attached to my sides. Fucking judgmental asshole.

My smile is so fake it kills me. "One moment please, sir. I just need to say bye to my boys." I go to face the boys but I can't. I have to say something right here, right now. For the little boy in me always doubted and deemed at fault, for the hundreds of others like me, and for the boys beside me living it in the present.

I hang my head for a moment to make sure that my composure is nothing less than respectful. And that in itself is a fucking feat. "Next time, sir, it'd be best to remember that Aiden is telling the truth. It's the bullies that need to be sent home, not good kids like Aiden here. He may not be perfect, but just because he doesn't come from a traditional home, doesn't mean that he's at fault." I stare at him, holding those flustered eyes of his as he listens—not just hears but listens—to the words I've said. When I see them register, I do the only disrespectful thing that I can and turn my back on him, dismissing him without further comment.

My smile changes from tight to genuine when I look at the three pairs of eyes looking up at me. It's one thing to stick up for them with bullies that are the same age, it's another thing when it's done to an adult. I understand that more than anyone.

"I don't think they'll be bugging you anymore, Aiden." I reach out and when I see his eyes accept my intention, ruffle his hair. "In fact, I don't think anyone will be bugging you guys anymore. If so, you let me know, okay?" All three boys nod like bobble-head dolls, their minds and egos trying to comprehend what's just happened.

"Time to get to class," Ry tells them as she steps up beside me to watch them walk toward the doors, heads held high and pride in their posture. They reach the door, looking the principal in the eye and that alone fills me with a sense of right. Ricky and Scooter disappear through the door, but Aiden stops.

I immediately worry that he fears entering the school—years of belittling not fixable with one appearance by a guy like me—but when he looks up, his eyes meet mine and I see awe, clear as day. "Thanks, Colton." I can't help the feeling that twists within me. Two simple words but the way he says them implies so much more.

Rylee glances over at me as we walk back to the car. Pride is brimming in her eyes, and I swear to God something shifts and twists inside of me. A fucking foreign feeling. But fuck if I don't want her to look at me like that again.

I get the boys understanding why I did what I did. But Rylee? She's got to be assuming things that I'd rather remain hidden. She's got to wonder what exactly it is that burns so deep within me that I still fear it every minute of every day. Even twenty-two years later.

Too bad she wasn't around to save me way back then.

The question is, *can she save me now?*

"Why did you agree to come here if you don't like coffee?" That in itself says volumes to me.

She denied me at the track even though her body said otherwise. I got a ration of shit from the guys for her being there too. They're not used to a woman walking away when I ask her to stay. They thought it was the funniest fucking thing on the face of the earth, Rylee denying me.

And her reason for having to get the boys was a bullshit excuse. That much I know.

So she must be scared. Fuck, I'd be scared too after the shit I've pulled with her. Back and forth like a goddamn tennis match because my head's so fucked-up that I want her but know I can't give her what she needs.

The fucking problem is my wants are changing and I'm not sure just yet how to deal with that. Because I don't want them to change. So I let her in more than anyone I ever have and then lash out because I can't deal with the shit her being around churns up. The vulnerability of my past being exposed, my demons reawakened.

And yet she still called me when she needed help. Fuck if that call didn't surprise me, but blowing off the Penzoil rep was worth it to be standing beside her right now.

Trying to figure out what the hell I'm doing because fuck if I know.

I study her profile, a soft smirk on her face as she contemplates my question while staring at the muffins in the glass case in front of us. She's pretending to decide what to order, but I can tell she's figuring out how to answer me. With honesty because despite the smiles on our faces there is still an underlying tension of unanswered questions between us, or with humor to try and add some levity.

Pick, Ryles. Set the tone for the rest of this conversation because I'm sure as fuck uncertain where to go from here.

"I may not like the coffee part, but Starbucks has some damn good food that is oh-so bad for you."

You have no idea how true that statement is, sweetheart. I shake my head, my smile more genuine now but her comment weaving into my thoughts. Telling me that she gets this. Gets that anything between us will be a beautiful disaster.

We move up in line, and I can hear the comments starting behind me and at the tables around us. My name is a hushed murmur and usually I'm cool with the attention, but right now I need it to be her and me. I need to figure out why I keep coming back to something that we both know is going to happen again, but this time I fear will either break me or devastate her.

And that's a heavy fucking burden for a man to bear. I'd like to say I'll walk away right now and save her the pain but know sure as shit—because I'm standing here—that I can't. I'd like to think I'd sacrifice myself, take the hit my own demons will hand me, but fuck, I know how brutal that would be.

I'm not sure if I'm willing to face them in order to let this thing with her play out. And I know that makes me a man weaker than most but hell if I want to relive the horror that's robbed my soul more than once in a lifetime.

But then again why in the hell am I even wasting time thinking shit like this that I'm never going to allow. Love's not a possibility for me. Relationships have strings and expectations. Those are hard limits I won't cross, can't cross.

And yet here I am, curious what it is about her that I just can't let go.

"What wo-would you l-like?" The barista stammers when she recognizes me as we step up and thank fuck for that because she pulls me from all of the crap I am overthinking.

Fucking Rylee is rubbing off on me with her reading too much into shit. I can think of other things I'd like to rub off on when it comes to her.

The image that flashes in my head is so very welcome and makes me chuckle and shake my head. I think the cashier catches the suggestive tone of my laugh and infers the direction of my thoughts because she blushes. She busies herself with the cashier buttons as she takes our order and I can't resist, as we walk away I make sure to say thanks and wink before flashing a huge grin.

We're lucky to find a table in the corner since the place is packed, and I enjoy the view of Ry's ass when I pull her chair out before I sit down myself. We sit and stare at each other for a few moments, smirks on our faces and questions in our eyes.

"You know that after what you did today, you've most likely reached idol status with the boys now."

I roll my eyes at her. A hero, I'm far fucking from that. If she knew what I was thinking in line, she'd see I'm more a coward than anything. Idols don't hide in corners when monsters enter the room to steal things from them that can never be replaced. They fight back, they overcome, they escape and save the fucking day—not cower and cry and plead when pain is headed their way.

They don't need to call to superheroes because they become one themselves.

I can't answer her because I know the truth, so I avert my gaze and focus way too intensely on the muffin in my hand. I take a bite, pushing the ghosts back in their closet and finally look up to see her eyes fixed on where I just licked a crumb from my lip.

My thoughts vanish instantly as my dick stands up and takes notice of her physical reaction. She lifts her eyes to mine and we stare at each other for a moment, the buzz of the coffee shop allowing a comfortable silence between us despite the unspoken desire in both of our eyes.

"Ace." The barista calls my name and unknowingly breaks our connection. I stand to get my coffee and smile at Rylee, letting her know this visual conversation is far from over. And hopefully my vision will get the sight of her naked and beneath me sooner rather than later.

The thought occupies my mind as I doctor my coffee and the

need to have her again only intensifies as I sit back down in front of her. I take a sip, the drink scalding my tongue. "Now I can think clearly."

And sitting here with her in front of me and the boys' status redeemed at school causes all kinds of clarity. Like how I sure as fuck want to let her in a bit, see where this takes us.

I'm not sure how to do it or where to go from here.

I've got a whole cup of coffee to figure it out, though, and time's a wasting.

FUELED WITH DESIRE,
CRASHING INTO LOVE

Fueled

BOOK TWO

K. BROMBERG

NEW YORK TIMES BESTSELLING AUTHOR

Fueled

Chapter Three.Five

Haddie's *game changer* conversation with Colton on the phone is probably one of the most requested scenes from FUELED to be written from Colton's perspective.

I enjoyed trying to figure out what was going on in his mind when he dealt with Haddie and her pull-no-punches attitude. I laughed at his reaction when he finds out Rylee is out drinking tequila.

We all rooted for Haddie in this scene in the original version, but this one adds a bit more to it when we know what exactly Colton was thinking.

WHY DOES IT FUCKING MATTER?

I pace the confines of the greenroom, restless and on edge.

Why should I care if she's watching or not?

"Ten minutes, Colton."

I whirl around at Kimmel's production assistant peeking her face through the doorway, agitation giving way to aggravation. I just grunt a response, too wrapped up in my own goddamn head to say anything else.

Fuck! I wish I could yell it out! Get the pent up bullshit off of my chest. But I don't. Can't. It's my own damn fault. My own fucked-up head ruling my life.

I've got to get it together and soon before I walk out on stage and make a fool of myself because my head is wrapped around something else. Someone else. Just like I wish my body was.

Fucking Rylee.

I shouldn't.

I should.

I shouldn't.

Aw, fuck it!

My fingers are dialing before I even give myself a chance to stop.

What the fuck am I doing? I want this but I don't. Need her but don't want to need her. Whiplash is an understatement to describe the fucking tug-of-war raging inside of me right now.

Man the fuck up, Donavan. Grab your balls back and put them firmly in place. Wanting to fuck her is okay. You're calling because that's all you want to do. Nothing else. You don't need her. You don't need anyone.

I keep repeating the words to myself, the lie so ludicrous no way in hell I'd even convince Baxter of it. *Fuck.* I'm about done with the pussification of my thoughts, finger hovering over the end call button when music blasts on the other line. I freeze.

"Rylee's phone can I help you?"

I can barely hear her voice above the music and I'm immediately irked. And then I'm pissed at myself for even caring when I shouldn't be because she doesn't even really matter in the first place. Nice try, Donavan. Keep telling yourself that and you just might believe it.

"I'm looking for Ry. It's Colton."

"*Who?*" she shouts and I wince from the sound coming through the phone.

"Colton." My patience is about to run out. Why the fuck is Ry not answering her phone? And where exactly the hell are they?

"Who? Oh hey, Colby!"

What? I stop pacing and grit my teeth. What the fuck is going on here? "*Who's Colby?*"

"Oh, I'm sorry. I thought you were Colby."

"Not hardly," I say, jaw clenched, anger bristling. Whoever the fuck Colby is, he's going to wish he wasn't Colby if I find him trying to talk to Ry again.

But this is just for sex. Yeah, that's it.

"*Who?*"

And now I feel like I'm being fucked with. Does Ry not talk about me? Does whoever this person that's close enough she trusts to answer her phone not know who I am? Impossible.

You called pit stop, fucker. *No rings, no strings.* She can do what-the-fuck-ever she wants. So why do I want to punch the mirror in front of me?

I force a swallow down my throat, hating that I care if she's talking about me and hating that I don't care even more. Fucking Christ. I've been voodooed. Fucking sucked in by her magic and I never even knew it.

Uneasiness and disbelief crawls up my spine. I shake it off. No fucking way. There's no way I've been taken by her goddamn pussy. Time to prove it.

"Colton Donavan," I say, authority in my voice. Time to quit playing fucking games here.

"Oh, hiya, Colton, this is Haddie. Rylee's roommate."

Thank Christ, we're finally getting somewhere. "Hi, Haddie. I need to talk to Rylee." Need to? Why the fuck did I say I need to? I don't need anything from her.

"Mmm-hmm. Well look, she's a little drunk right now and a lot busy, so she can't talk to you, but I'd like to."

Drunk? *Rylee?* In a club on a weeknight? I'm so not liking the images in my head right now. Images like the fucking commercial I'm about to debut. Bodies grinding. Hands groping. Sexy clothes.

I can't help the groan that falls from my mouth and fuck if Haddie doesn't hear it because she laughs at me. Fucking laughs. I grind my molars and hope no one is grinding on Ry right now.

"So here's the deal. I don't know you very well, but from what I do, you seem like a decent guy. A little too much in the press from your shenanigans if you ask me as you make jobs like mine a little harder, but hey, no press is bad press, right? But I digress ..."

"Thanks for the PR consult. Don't think I asked." I roll my shoulders as I look at the signatures of past guests on the walls and shake my head in frustration. Be nice. She's the only way you're going to find out what the fuck is going on. "Are you guys having something to drink with dinner?" I seriously just asked that? *Fish much, Donavan?* And then that laugh of hers again as if the joke's on me.

Fuckin' A.

"Wine for starters, but now we've moved on to shots. Tequila. Anyway, I just wanted to tell you that you really need to get your shit together when it comes to Rylee."

Wait a minute. *Tequila?* Images flash in my head of the last time I saw Ry doing a shot of that shit. It was after she left me at the Merit Rum party. Stood at the bar, downed the shot like a goddamn pro, and then ran from me. My dick pulses at the memory of what came next though: possession, claiming, some of the best fucking sex of my life.

"Yes, I was talking to you, Colton." She misunderstands my silence. Must think I'm not listening but instead am thinking of what it was like to see Rylee naked for the first time. Soft skin. Perfect fucking tits. Sinking into her. Hearing that sigh? Goddamn perfection.

So why the fuck is she in some club and not here with me? Because I called a damn pit stop. Motherfucker. I shake my head, the barrage of questions I want to ask fill my head but never have the chance to come out.

"I. Said. You. Need. To. Get. Your. Shit. Together," Haddie repeats, annoyance and don't-fuck-with-my-friend in her tone. But hell yeah, I want to fuck her friend. I start to speak, shout at her so she can hear me above that goddamn music, but she cuts me off.

"Rylee's a game changer, babe. You better not let her slip through your fingers or someone else is going to snatch her right out from under your nose. And from the looks of the sharks circling tonight, you better kick that fine ass of yours into high gear."

Sweet Christ! This is a one way conversation and yet I've just been knocked speechless. *Sharks circling.* Those fucking innocent eyes of hers and body that screams of sin put on display for others to watch. To touch. To want.

Fuck. Me.

"Where are you guys?" I'm about ready to blow off Kimmel, repercussions be damned. "Where?" I demand again.

"Like I said, she's quite busy right now choosing which guy will buy her next drink, but I'll let her know you called."

"Goddammit, Haddie! Where the fuck are you?" I bite the words out, ready to leave. To go get her. Claim her. Anything just so I can feel her again. Can have the peace she brings me again.

Because this is just fucking. That's all it is.

I shake my head and talk to Haddie as if I'm fucking trying to persuade myself. "You know what? I don't care where you guys are. She's a big girl. Can do her own thing." Jesus Christ, if you're gonna lie, at least make it sound convincing.

"Uh-huh, yes. I know, but I just thought you ought to know. Game. Changer," she says, like I'm a fucking two-year-old. As if I don't already know it. As if I didn't already cause this fucking situation because I called a pit stop to convince myself otherwise.

"Oh and, Colton? If you make her fall, you better make damned certain you catch her. Hurting her is not an option. Understood? Because if you do hurt her, you'll have to answer to me, and I can be a raving bitch!" Her taunting laugh fills the line. "Good night, Colton. I hope to see you around once you figure your shit out. Cheers!"

I go to speak, to participate in the conversation that's just fucked with my head more than it already is, and I hear a goddamn dial tone. What the fuck? Did I actually just get an ultimatum? As if I don't know I have shit to figure out.

I stare at myself in the mirror as I toss my phone on the counter and shake my head at my reflection.

Fucking hell.

Game changer? Like I didn't already know that.

Goddamn women.

I roll my shoulders and audibly exhale.

Holy shit … I've been voodooed.

What the fuck am I going to do about it now?

Fueled

Between Chapter Five and Chapter Six

The bromance between Colton and Becks is a favorite of many. We first see it begin to emerge in FUELED when they are at the bar before the Las Vegas trip. This scene is a short one I wrote for the moment that Becks realizes Colton wasn't lying, that they really are bringing Rylee to the City of Sin with them.

"IS THERE A REASON SAMMY is driving in the opposite direction of the airport?"

I need another beer. Need something to help numb the nonsense in my head telling me I really want this. Want her.

Fucking Rylee.

"I'm not *that* drunk. I do know the difference between east and west," Becks says as he tips his own bottle back again. "You can't pull one over on me."

"She's got a hot friend," I repeat, hoping the idea will shut him the fuck up and let me enjoy my buzz.

"Her ass better be fucking blazing and her tits better be perfection if you're actually dragging women—*walking vaginas*—to Vegas with us … land of free-balling, free-wheeling, *The Hangover* fucked-up-ness. Seriously, dude? You've lost your fucking marbles. Or handed over your balls." He shrugs with a chuckle. "They're about the same size."

"Fuck off, Daniels." I grunt at him as I lay my head back, the black interior of the limo all starting to fuse together as it spins like a fucking car doing donuts on the track.

Or the Tilt-A-Whirl at the carnival with Rylee.

How I wouldn't like to take her for a spin right now.

"Fucker? Are you listening to me?" Becks's voice breaks through my thoughts. The ones Rylee commandeers even when she's not even around.

"Yeah, what?" I angle my head over so that I can see him. "I was just thinking about … *stuff.*"

"Dude, get the voodoo pussy out of your head for a second."

"Becks, there's nothing more I'd like right now than to have my head in her wet, willing voodoo."

"You are a disappointment to all men! Not only did you break the no barebacking pact, but you are fucking grinning about it."

"I need another beer if I have to listen to your whiny ass. Shit, we're going to the City of Sin and I'm putting a hottie on your arm … so quit your bitching, pact broken or not."

"I *know* you're riding without a saddle now because it's obviously fucking with your head," he says, holding up his hands to stop the retort he knows from years of friendship is on my tongue. The one about how much I want one of my two heads fucked with.

"Really chaps your hide, doesn't it," I say, fighting the laugh I want to release because fuck, even if I'm well on my way to getting drunk, I still know that was pretty damn witty.

"Fucking hilarious," he says sarcastically, shaking his head. "*Sooooo* … how are you going to handle Vegas with a chick on your arm?"

I'm instantly irritated at the comment. And now I'm wondering why. What is it about what Becks says that angers me?

"Don't look at me like that!" he says, and I can tell he's getting into Becks-knows-all mode. *Fuck!* I so don't need this right now. "Vegas is usually a flesh feast, so tell me how that's going to go over with Wonder-Rylee there? Did you think of that, cowboy?"

I close my eyes and emit a sliver of a laugh. "The only all-you-can-eat-buffet I'll be fucking dining at will be Ry's Thighs." I quirk my eyebrows up at him, challenge given. Got a comeback to that one now, fucker? "Besides, I wouldn't doubt she'd throw down if someone got in her way. She fights for what's hers."

And the words are out there before I can fucking take them back. Goddamn alcohol in my brain.

"*What's hers?* Did you just officially acknowledge—admit—what-the-fuck-ever that you're taken?" Becks spits out his beer. "Stop the car, Sammy!" he yells.

The limo swerves quickly to the side of the road and stops with a jerk. I know Sammy thinks Becks is gonna hurl. Did he really drink that fucking much? *Lightweight.*

Becks opens the door beside him and climbs out. "Hey, Wood?"

I'm confused by the amusement in his voice when he's supposed to be getting sick. "Yeah?" I ask as I angle my head out to look at him, beer in hand, lights from passing cars flashing over his face.

"Feel that?" he says, lifting his face up to the sky. "That's the fucking arctic chill right there!"

"What the fuck are you talking about?" He's starting to ruin my buzz here so I'm getting pissed.

"Dude, you're barebacking, we're taking chicks to Vegas with us, and that has to mean Hell is most definitely freezing over. What in the fuck is this world coming to?"

I just shake my head at him. "Get in the car, Beckett. If I'm gonna be around a pussy, it sure as fuck needs to be one I can get enjoyable use out of ... and you, my friend, are being one but hell if I'd enjoy you."

He slides in the car next to me and just stares at me, a smirk on his mouth and amusement in his eyes.

Me and my fucking mouth.

"Okay, Sam, we're good to go!" Becks says with a chuckle, and the car starts to take off.

I open the top of another beer. I think I'm going to need this to deal with him tonight. *I'm not fucking hers.* Becks is just out if his damn mind if he thinks I'm a kept man.

I'll tire of her. I always do. Shit, one woman isn't going to be able to change my MO. There's not enough game in the world that can change this player.

We drive for a bit, both of us staring out the window to the world beyond until he finally breaks the silence. *"Really?"* he asks with a shake of his head, meeting my eyes. And I know what he's asking. Are you sure? Is she really worth it? Is Rylee really going to Vegas with us?

Is she the real-deal voodoo?

I purse my lips for a second and nod my head. "Damn straight, she is."

Fueled

Chapter Twenty-Two and a Half

Here is a new chapter from FUELED. Rylee received the extremely 'romantic' poems that Colton composed in Nashville, but this scene takes you to how exactly those poems came about. A bit more bromance here, but also the reason behind Colton's slip the next morning when he casually called Rylee his girlfriend. I hope you enjoy this new piece of the puzzle.

"YOU KNOW WHAT I THINK?"

"Huh?" I look over to where Becks is sitting on the chair across from me, but I move too fast and the room spins for a minute before I can focus again.

"I think," he says, laughing and tilting God knows what number beer we're on at me, "I think we need to have a moment of silence."

"*Who died?*" I'm drunker than I thought. What did I miss? I lift my bottle to my lips and try to figure out what he's talking about.

"Your single, non-pussy-whipped self."

"Bullshit!" I spout through his damn laughter that's a little too loud right now for my drunk ears.

"*Bullshit?*" he says as he scoots to the edge of his chair, and I want to tell him not to stand, that he'll fall on his ass. Then again, he's fucking with me and I could use a good laugh at his expense so I refrain. "Were you just not looking at your phone like you wanted to call her and get off?"

I lay my head back and laugh because hell if he's not right. It's been five fucking days since I've had her, since she stayed the weekend at my place. Hours occupied with sex that rocked my world and downtime where she challenged me, pushed me, laughed with me. A first for me on so many levels, but the most important one was that I wasn't freaked the fuck out about it.

And that never happens.

"It's called Skype," I tease, closing my eyes momentarily. No amount of alcohol can fuck with the perfect image in my head of answering my iPad to find Rylee sitting on her bed, lace and garters and come-fuck-me-gear on the other end of the picture connection. Manicured fingernails parting pink flesh to show me just what I'm missing. Dirty talk I'd never expect to fall from her lips but perfectly fitting in that telephone-sex rasp of hers.

"*Exactly.* When have you ever had Skype-sex? You usually snap your fingers in whatever town you're in and you can pick from the hundred that come running and drop to their knees." I hear the pop of a bottle top and then another and open my eyes to see him holding a fresh one out to me.

I think for a second as I accept it and fuck if he's not right.

"See? *I told you.* When you brought her to Vegas with us I thought she was just a passing fad. Thought you were testing the waters because you weren't used to having a challenge and it got a rise out of you. *Literally,*" he deadpans, drawing a shake of my head. "But, Wood, after the past few weeks, you bailing from work early to go to go-kart tracks and shit … It's more than obvious that we need to say our parting words and have a moment of silence for your dearly departed dick."

"Becks—"

"Shh!" he responds, trying to hold his pointer finger to his lips but his depth perception is so off I laugh when he tries several times to get it there despite his dead serious face. "A moment of silence is needed to kiss your unvoodooed ass goodbye."

"You're such an asshole," I tell him but know I'm lucky to have him as my partner in crime.

"Shh!" he says again, and I give up. I take a deep breath and roll my eyes but humor him and remain silent. I swear he's passed out but he's still sitting at the edge of the chair and hasn't fallen over.

Yet.

But his eyes are still closed when a huge-ass grin turns his mouth up and he claps his hands together and rubs them. "Shit, that was easier than I thought."

"What was?" My buzz is humming now and I'm finally relaxed after a fuck-all day with the Firestone guys and negotiations over shit they're going to cave on in the end anyway.

"Getting you to admit you're a kept man now."

"Fucking Christ, dude!" I spit my beer out. "Kept? You're calling me kept?" That's like the equivalent of telling Jenna Jameson she's a virgin.

"It's pretty fucking obvious when there's a huge neon sign above your head flashing no vacancy for your stabbin' cabin that you're a kept man. Have a woman now."

"A woman now? I'm sure Ry would love to hear you refer to her as that."

He eyes me over his bottle. "So she's not your woman, then? Because usually when you hang up the phone you don't think twice, back to business. Now you hang up with a little smirk on your face and you're lost in la-la land for a bit."

"La-la land?" I laugh.

"What would you call it, then? Girlfriend-ville?" He eyes me. Dares me to deny his reference since I'm the self-proclaimed *don't do the girlfriend thing* kind of guy.

I begin to argue but then stop. *Fucking Becks.* He knows me like the back of my hand and yet this is uncharted fucking territory for me. A woman that I want to color outside the lines with. No, scratch that. A woman that fucks with me on so many levels that I'm so busy being challenged and seduced by her words, her body, and her defiance that I don't even realize the parameters I'm used to controlling don't really matter anymore … because she does.

Fuckin' A, he's right, but hell if I'll tell him that.

"We'll go with *woman*," I concede, but the word *girlfriend* rolls around in my head, sticking here and there as I get used to the idea of it.

"Holy shit!" Becks says, pounding on his chest acting like he's choking and I just stare at him unamused despite the smile on my lips. He stops laughing and tosses a bottle cap at me as he leans back in his chair. "Well, admission is half the battle. Keeping her is the other half."

"Keeping her?" Dude's got my head spinning. I mean, fuck, I just told her I'd try, asked her to spend the weekend at Broadbeach with me when no one ever has, and he's talking about how to keep her? I didn't realize she was going somewhere.

"Baby steps, Becks. Don't give me a heart attack here. I hear keeping her but I think rings and strings and weddings and shit."

And he only thinks my reaction makes the whole situation funnier by how he curls up and can't stop laughing. "The look on your face is priceless," he finally gets out, "but I'm not talking about marriage."

Thank fuck for that. We can put away the defibrillators now. I look over at him, eyes telling him to get to the fucking point so I can enjoy my beer again without any more cardiac arrests.

"I'm talking about romance. Shit girls like, man."

"You don't need romance when you have my skills," I tell him, already waiting for the smart-ass comment to come from his mouth.

"Okay, *one-pump chump*."

"Fuck off!" I sneer and flip my middle finger up, but he's laughing so hard he doesn't even see it.

"Shit. I've got to take a piss," he says and rises on unsteady feet to head to the bathroom of my suite.

I lift my feet up and prop them on the table in front of me, hands clasped behind my head. Through the open balcony doors I can hear Bruno Mars's newest song playing in the bar across the street, but in the muted silence I start thinking about the word girlfriend. Wondering if that's a definition we really need when we have our own language between us. Then Beckett's words start running over again in my head until he comes back out zipping up his fly.

He walks over to the open doors and I feel a slight pang of guilt that he wanted to go hang out at the bar and I just didn't want to deal with the crowd tonight. I'm usually interested in the eye candy and playing the game.

But I just don't feel like it this trip.

I shake my head. What in the fuck is Rylee doing to me? All her talk about Scooter saying I *Spiderman you* and that look on her face as she sat naked on her knees beside me undoes me bit by bit when I'm already a mess of unraveled memories.

I lean forward and grab another beer from the bucket of ice in front of me and stare at the label for a few minutes. "So uh, romance, huh?"

I see his body register my words, but he keeps his face toward the street because he can tell I'm so far out of my fucking element here, the periodic table wouldn't even be able to help me.

Romance? I don't do it. Flowers die, food gets eaten. It's not real. I've watched people flip the switch on and off enough in my life between my dad's movie sets to women wanting something with me that I'm not fucking stupid enough to see the farce.

So why the fuck am I wondering what Becks thinks I'm screwing up here?

"What are you not saying to me? You think I'm not giving her the flowery shit a girl wants so she's gonna bail?" The thought doesn't settle well in my stomach. In fact it makes me shove up out of my chair and walk back and forth.

Well more like stumble.

"I didn't say shit, dude." Becks keeps looking out the window. He knows he's questioned me and I don't take too easy to that.

And fuck if he doesn't have me questioning myself now. I told her I'd try to give her more. That has to be enough in the end here. I'm already pushing myself past my comfort zone and now I have to think about this kind of shit?

I'm annoyed with Becks for butting his nose in and irritated at myself for not even thinking about it. But I shouldn't have to, should I?

I roll my shoulders and plop back down on the couch. Did he really have to ruin my stellar buzz by bringing this up? Then again, the room's still moving a bit so maybe he didn't.

"What do you think I should do? Send her poems and shit? C'mon, dude, that's not me."

He snorts out a laugh. "Yeah. I'm sure a classy 'roses are red' poem is just what a lady like her wants."

I sit there in silence, ignoring the dig, thoughts running through my semi-cloudy mind and plaster a grin to my face when the words connect. "Roses are red, tires are black, you're the only pussy I wanna ride bareback."

Becks spits out the beer in his mouth in a huge spray out the balcony doors. He wipes his mouth as his laughter falls to match mine. He turns to face me and raises an eyebrow. "That was pretty fucking good. If you're that witty when you're drunk, I think we should work under the influence more often." He walks toward me and I can already see his mind turning, trying to match my poem. "I've got one. Roses are red, violets are fine, you be the six, and I'll be the nine."

"Now that's a good image to have," I say, my mind immediately back on her in that fucking outfit from Skype.

"Down, boy. Poetry, not pornography," he says, tapping the neck of his bottle against mine before sitting back in his chair. "Not with me anyway."

"No worries there. You're cute and all but not my type." I lean back and fall into thought before I start laughing. Look at us. Two guys in our thirties making up fucking nursery rhymes. This is some funny shit.

Becks chuckles to himself, his eyes closed, and I wait for him to speak. "Roses are red, violets are blue, get in my bed and be ready to screw."

"How fucked-up are we?" I laugh.

"Hey, this is poetry in its truest form." He lifts his beer to me, his eyes still closed as the alcohol mixed with the clock hitting past midnight begins to get to him. "In fact, you should send her one of them tomorrow. That's something a good *boyfriend* would do."

"You and your boyfriend bullshit," I tell him, taking my hat off and tossing it on the table. "I'm so good, dude, labels like that don't apply to me."

"Oh Jesus." He throws his hands up, his beer splashing up the top of his longneck that has him sputtering to wipe it off his shirt. "Forgive me, Oh-King-of-All-Things in his own mind."

"Damn straight," I say, loving to get his feathers ruffled.

"Let me ask you something," Becks says as he props his feet on the table. "Do you fuck her regularly?"

I nearly spit my beer out but don't because I may be feeling more than good, but no one talks about Ry this way. I make sure my eyes tell him exactly that.

"Oh, excuse me, choirboy Colton. Let me rephrase. Are you having *regular relations* with her?" he asks in a prim and proper voice.

I can't help but laugh. *Fucker.* He just stares at me, eyebrows raised, waiting for me to answer. "Every chance I get."

He nods his head and works his tongue in his mouth while he thinks. "What's she doing tonight?"

What's up with the questions? "She was at The House until nine and then heading to dinner with Haddie. Why?"

"So you know her schedule then?"

"And your point is …?" He's starting to irritate me with this cryptic bullshit.

"When's her birthday?" He ignores my question by asking another, a regular fucking Socrates.

"September fifteenth." Becks chuckles and I blow out an exhale at the condescending sound of it.

"Impressive." He nods his head in approval. "Now I know you'll know her bra size, but what about her shoe size?"

"What the fuck dude? What are you getting at?"

"Patience, young grasshopper. Bra and shoe size?"

"I'll *young grasshopper* your ass if you don't get to the fucking point."

He leans forward and lifts a beer from the bucket toward me in offering. I nod my head and take it. Fuck it. I might as well answer him than deal with his crap. Besides, I've gotta admit I'm curious where he's going with this. "Thirty Six D and size nine and half."

"Nice," Becks says, drawing it out in a sound of approval. "What are her parents' names?"

"Daniels," I grit out, patience lost amidst his amusing twenty questions.

"Last one, I promise." He puts his hands up in surrender.

"Mr. and Mrs. Thomas." *Take that.* I can be a smart ass just like you.

"Just answer." He sighs in exasperation.

"If I answer, are you going to get to your point?" He nods his head, his grin spreading even wider as I tell him their names.

"Huh."

"Huh?" After all the build up, that's all he's going to give me? I lean forward and rest my elbows on my knees waiting for an answer.

He angles his head and looks me in the eyes for a beat. And despite the spinning in my head, curiosity is killing the cat. And of course cat leads me to thinking of pussy and pussy to Rylee. *Fuck.* I'm definitely drunk.

"Boyfriend," he says, breaking through my thoughts, know-it-all grin spreading from ear to ear.

"*Fuck off.*" It's the only comeback I have because he just baited the hook and I thought he was going to tell me something unexpected. What an ass. I throw the pillow beside me at him and flop back on the cushions.

He catches it and laughs loudly. "Those are things boyfriends know. Not fuck buddies, not random assholes—although, you qualify for the asshole part too—but boyfriends."

"Isn't it time you head back to your room? Isn't your hand and some lotion waiting for you there?"

"Best offer I've had all night," he says, pushing himself up off the couch, and I laugh when it takes him a moment to steady his feet. "I think I'll try to enjoy it before I pass the fuck out ..."

"You go do that," I tell him, slipping my shoes off and turning my feet so I can lift them onto the couch and lie down. "Tell Rosy and Palmela to do you right," I tease, making the jerking-off motion with my free hand.

"No worries, they never disappoint," he says and so many comebacks flicker in my mind but are just beyond my drunken haze so I nod my head instead. "You just lie there and enjoy thinking about the sex you have regularly now with the woman you claim isn't your girlfriend but who really is." He opens the door. "Catch ya in the morning, *boyfriend.*"

Asshole is the word that comes to mind but all I say is, "Hmm …" as the door clicks shut and my eyelids begin to feel heavy. I start to doze, my mind on Rylee, wondering if the boys were good during her shift today. If she made it home okay afterwards. Shit! I'm thinking about stuff I normally don't give a flying fuck about … stuff a *boy-friend* would think about.

There's that fucking word again.

Thoughts come and go but they're all focused on the one person I never expected to be thinking about. The damn voodoo she's grabbed me by the balls with and is now somehow twisting around my hard-ened heart.

… If you were one of my boys and you wanted to tell me you loved me, or vice versa, you'd say 'I race you, Rylee'…

The words flicker through my buzzed mind. I try to shake them, try to forget that look in her eyes when she made the statement. Try to focus on the incredible sex we had afterward.

But as I fall asleep on the couch in some overpriced hotel suite in Nashville, my mind should be focused on tomorrow's negotiations and the upcoming season. I should be dreaming of great sex with a hot blonde.

But I'm not.

I'm thinking of roses and violets, of *my girlfriend,* and learning that maybe Spiderman and racing off the track just might have a thing or two in common.

Fueled

Chapter Thirty-Eight

The well-loved hotel fight scene in FUELED. What did Colton think when he saw Rylee with Parker in the bar? Was he trying to fix things or looking to make it worse? Why in the hell did he tell her he slept with Tawny? Why did he shut Becks the hell up so the misunderstanding couldn't be resolved?

Yes, Colton was an ass for kissing that girl so blatantly in front of Rylee earlier in the night, but at the same time I feel for him in this scene. When he stands in front of Rylee and Parker and silently asks her the same thing she asked him about Raquel at the Merit Rum party: choose.

As usual Colton is all over the place mentally and emotionally, but we also see something else here: We see defeat and desperation. Two things that as a reader calls to my sympathy, my compassion, my desire to see them figure it all out … and possibly makes his earlier actions more tolerable.

"I TOLD YOU, BECKS, I'M sick of her shit. I'm not buying the *I'm inno-cent* act she pulled in the team meeting." I glance over to him as we walk down the hallway, enough alcohol humming through my veins for me to speak my mind.

Then again, I don't need alcohol to do that.

"What the fuck did Tawny do now?"

"I don't know, man, but she's being squirrely and fuck if I can figure out what she's up to."

Sammy snorts behind me and I turn to look at him, figure what the hell he means by it, but he just looks right past me like it's not his place to say anything. Ha. Like he's held back before.

Becks catches my eye with his raised brows as we turn a corner because I'm heading in the opposite direction of our wing of rooms for the team. "You can deal with it when we get back home. I need your head focused on the race."

"No shit, Sherlock." I shake my head, eyes scanning over all of the places I've seen Rylee since she's arrived. I need to see her, need to set the shit right that I did earlier. My dumb-ass move to kiss bar-girl just to make Rylee jealous, show her that I can have anybody I want.

Even though it's her I want.

So I hurt her on purpose as a payback for her twisting the knife a little more every time I see her. Sitting at appearances, promoting the fundraiser—everything beside me—but the minute the attention is off of us, she disengages. Goddamn frustrating woman.

So why are you looking for her, then? Why do you still care, Donavan? She doesn't believe a fucking word you say, said she's done, so how are you going to prove otherwise?

Fuck if I know but I'm so sick of this ache in my chest that I'm trying to ignore regardless of how much it continues to burn.

"So you ever going to tell me what the fuck happened between you and Rylee? Why you're moping around like I kicked your dog?" Becks asks for the hundredth time, even though he knows Baxter would bite his ass if he kicked him.

I don't want to talk about this. Never do. I just want it all back how it was. Ry and me in a good place. Then why the fuck did you kiss that chick? Pull your head out and fight for what you want.

I glance over and Becks is giving me the look like he's waiting for an answer. My head's so fucked-up right now I forgot to respond.

"Nothing. Something." I exhale. "She thinks I cheated on her."

Becks starts laughing and pats me on the back. "Dude, does she not see how goddamn pussy whipped you are? I saw you shove Tawny off you like a hot fucking coal that night she kissed you." He laughs at the memory that caused the *morning after* that still haunts me. When Tawny opened the fucking door when Rylee knocked. "If you're not having your fallback girl, you sure as hell aren't locking lips—or anything else for that matter—with anyone else."

I sigh, that ache returning with a vengeance.

"It'll sort itself out as long as you don't go and do something stupid, Wood."

"I won't," I lie, then cringe at the memory of Rylee's eyes filled with hurt as I *locked lips* with that bimbo earlier. Fuckin' A.

"Because she sure as hell wouldn't do something stupid like …" Becks's words trail off as we pass the bar before he takes an abrupt turn down the hall in the opposite direction. I start to follow when I see him glance at Sammy. I stop and turn around, the unspoken words causing the heart I've thought dead for so long to roar to life.

I see her instantly, body turned, knees touching, and face close to some fucking douchebag sitting beside her in the bar. I freeze for a moment when I see her leaning forward. *The kiss I see is all in my fucked-up mind* but I don't fucking care because I see it anyway, feel it hit me like a goddamn sucker punch. Just like she must have felt when I did it to her earlier.

The hurt barrels through me. Grabs hold and doesn't let go.

And I don't allow myself to get hurt. *Ever.* I lived a lifetime of fucking pain caused by the one that was supposed to care about me the most. I know better now. Know that the minute someone gets too close, I push them away. The minute I feel like I'm going to be hurt, I lash out without regret.

… and I let Rylee in close enough to hurt me …

She senses me, looks up, and our eyes lock. I see defiance, finality, and fuck if I'm going to let that bastard sitting beside her reinforce it being there. She told me she was going to find a guy for the night to see if it helps with her pain. Apparently she was serious.

But this isn't like her—acting like me, throwing the confession I gave her about how I cope back in my face—so it kills me to see her do this to spite me. *To hurt me on purpose.*

Bar-boy leans in closer, his mouth near her ear, and she breaks her eyes from mine. And now that ache turns into motherfucking pain.

Defense mechanism locked and loaded. She's not going to believe me? Going to pull shit like this? I need to get back to *every man for his fucking self* ... well, after I take care of this I'll get right on that.

I'm ready to lash out and thank God the fucker sitting beside her is the perfect size for a punching bag because my fists are clenched and vision is red.

No one touches what's mine.

Even when she tells me she's not.

No one.

Things happen so fast. A shout sounds and I don't even realize it's mine until Becks is pushing my chest from the front and Sammy holds my shoulders from behind. It doesn't fucking matter who's on me because right now I want blood. I need an excuse to release my anger, at her for not believing me, at me for the stunt I pulled, and because I want to touch her so fucking badly it's not even funny.

And he's touching her instead.

"Let me go," I say through gritted teeth, trying to shrug them the fuck off of me. And I don't care how hard they hold me back because nothing is stopping me. I break free, Becks says something about priorities to which I think I only have one right now and that's getting this fucking guy away from her.

The crowd is smart and moves apart as I stalk toward her, mind focused, heart armoring up. She says something to the guy and stands as I near. Her eyes meet mine and they make me so fucking angry and so goddamn whipped that I push it away and focus on him.

If I was smart I'd haul her over my shoulder, take her upstairs and show her just exactly how I haven't cheated. But fuck smart and fuck being reasonable because she's being neither of those right now either.

Two wrongs don't make a right but hell if it doesn't feel good in the process.

I stop in front of her, lips so fucking close I can taste them, and she lifts that chin of hers up in a non-verbal *fuck you*. That defiance I find so goddamn sexy is in full effect but right now I'm also scared shitless because the hurt I see mixed with it is my doing ... and my undoing.

What the fuck am I doing?

My head is such a clusterfuck of emotions and thoughts. The biggest one is hurt her first. Deliver the first blow. And I know it's not right, know it's the worst kind of way to be, but my chest hurts so goddamn bad I can't think straight.

"What the fuck are you trying to pull, Rylee?" I ask. I know the answer, *payback's a bitch*, but I don't care because bar-boy shifts behind her and his eyes lock and then glance away from mine.

Good. At least he knows who's calling the shots here. Too bad Rylee doesn't.

And then she reaches back and pats his knee. I have flashbacks of the Merit launch party and Surfer Joe, the déjà vu almost comical.

Almost.

Because then she was just an addictive challenge I had to conquer and now ... now she's part of my fucking world. I'm a man with something to lose and that's not a good place to be.

"What business is it of yours?" she sneers as my eyes keep flickering back and forth to her hand on his knee.

And I can't help it, need to take it off of him, so I reach out to grab her arm and she yanks it away from me. I know why she did it, but the look she gives me mixed with the action flashes me back to my other hurt. When I fought away from any touch at all because of what would come next. The calling to my superheroes.

I'm staggered.

And fucking furious.

At her for fighting me and at me for making her feel *that* way. It takes a moment to pull me from the thought, to separate the two events that just melded when one has nothing to do with the other and fucked up my head even further.

I look in her eyes—see the hurt, the defiance, the sadness—and use what I see there to gain my bearings again.

"I don't like games, Rylee. I won't tell you that again."

"You don't like games?" she says, her tone laced with disgust. "But it's okay for you to play them?"

Fuck yes I played them, but that's not the point. The point is right here, right now. At the Merit party she gave me the choice: go or stay. Now it's my turn to ask.

"Why don't you tell your little boy toy he can run along now before things get even more interesting."

Watcha gonna do, Ryles?

Pick me.

Go with me.

Fix this shitstorm I started and get us back.

She shoves against me as hard as she can. "*You. Arrogant. Conceited. Egomaniac!*" spewing from her lips as she falls into me.

And every part of me stands at attention at the feel of her against me, wanting and needing but knowing I can't have, because she sure as fuck didn't give me the answer I wanted.

"What the fuck are you trying to prove?" I ask, wanting her to say she wants me, wants to fix this, believe I didn't cheat on her.

But she doesn't. Not even fucking close.

"I'm just testing your theory," she says with a smirk.

"My theory?" What the fuck is she talking about?

"Yeah, if losing yourself in someone helps get rid of the pain."

Ah fuck. In a single second I rein in everything that tumbles inside of me at the thought of her being with someone else, *everything but my anger.* I sure as shit hold onto that.

"How's that working for you?" It's all I can think to say because her rejection stings something fierce.

"Not sure." She shrugs with a smirk. "I'll let you know in the morning."

And I'm so focused on that look on her face when she pushes away from me that I don't even notice the fucker's hand in hers.

When I see it, anger turns to motherfucking fury. "Don't you walk away from me, Rylee!"

"You lost the right to tell me what to do the minute you slept with *her.*" She says, her voice breaking through the haze of my colliding emotions. "Besides, you said you like my ass … enjoy the view as I walk away because that's the last you'll be seeing of it."

I snap. No excuses, no regrets. My fist is clenched, fury ready to unleash on bar-boy.

But none of it fucking matters because I feel the steel grip of Sammy on my arm before I get my chance. And then the melee ensues.

Rylee is screaming at me, insults and names. Sticks and stones, baby. Sticks and stones.

You got to me.

You beat me at my own game.

At least it's Becks leading her away from me and not the fucking bar-boy. I'll take any kind of victory I can get at this point.

The crowd's buzzing seeps through my rage, drowns out her voice as it fades. And then Sammy's arm is around my shoulders leading me out of the bar and down a hallway.

"Calm the fuck down, Wood."

My pulse pounds in my ears, my head is all over the place, and my chest hurts even worse. "Just let me the fuck go, Sam," I grit out. My only thought is: Fuck the race tomorrow, I need to visit with Jack and Jim for a bit.

"Nope," he says, ushering me into an elevator in this damn maze of a resort. All I want to do is walk, run, pound out this anger then get fucking plastered so I can't feel the emptiness inside of me right now.

We're done.

She just made it clear as day and I don't want us to be done.

But it really doesn't fucking matter what I want or don't want because she doesn't fucking believe me. And why the fuck should she, Donavan, when you go kissing bimbos to spite her?

I groan and run a hand through my hair, fucking beside myself as Sammy pushes me out of the elevator car and down the hall.

"She's irrational and fuck she was going to sleep with that asshole and … motherfucker!" I shout into the hallway, not caring who the hell is asleep or if anyone is listening. I'm feeling everything all at once when I'm so fucking used to feeling nothing that I can't concentrate.

Anger vibrates through me.

My teeth grind. My hands fist. My blood pounding.

Fucking Rylee.

Sammy points to the door to his right and when I stop he puts both hands on my shoulders. "Get your fucking hands off of me, Sammy!"

He just laughs at me in that snarky way he has, and I've just add-ed him to the list of people I want to punch. Right after that fucking bar-boy he prevented me from plowing. I try to jerk my shoulders from his hands as he steers me down the hall, but I should know better by now. He's stronger than a fucking ox.

I'm so angry at him.

So pissed at her.

So disgusted with myself for the shit I pulled earlier without trying to make things right.

Rage blinds me and since every fucking room in this resort looks the same, I don't even realize what room Sammy shoves me into. By the time I look up, it's too fucking late.

"Uh-uh! No way! Get that egotistical asshole out of here!"

My head snaps up the minute I hear her voice. Sugar and spice laced together. Rage and lust and pure need collide momentarily until my mind flashes back to the image of Rylee with that fucker in the bar. The emotion hits me like a freight train.

I hate her.

I want her.

I hate that I want her so much that this is fucking killing me.

And she comes into view but without the dim light of the bar, I really see her. Hurt staining her face and defiance in her eyes, and I do the only thing I know how to do … push away the good and prepare for the pain. "Fuckin' A, Becks! What the fuck is this?" I yell, furious that I was coerced into a confrontation that I don't want. That I do want. *I don't know what the fuck I want because she doesn't want me anymore.*

I notice her packed suitcase and my heart fucking constricts in my chest. She's leaving me? The part of me that hoped this was all just a show dies a fast fucking death. And I thought her always saying she'd stay meant she would. That she understood I'd push and hurt to prove otherwise. I guess she doesn't understand me as much as I thought she did.

I say the only thing I can to hide the hurt lancing through me, to lash out. To hide the unexpected let down that drops through my soul knowing she doesn't want to be here and watch me chase the green flag tomorrow.

I confessed that I use pleasure to bury the pain … but fuck, right now, I'm about to use anger to hide the foreshadowed devastation.

"Thank Christ! *Don't let the door hit you in the ass, sweetheart!*"

She steps toward me and I can see the fire in her eyes, the fury in her lips, and that goddamn defiance in her posture. That defiance that makes me ache to take her like no other fucking woman I've ever met before, ever had before.

"This is over here and now!" Beckett's voice booms at us in a tone I've heard very few times during our friendship. Instinct has me turning to look at him because last time I heard him like this he threw a punch at me. I don't need this shit right now. Not Becks pissed and sure as hell not him interfering. "I don't care if I have to lock you in this fucking room together, but you two are going to figure your shit out or you're not leaving. Is that understood?"

I start to argue with him the same time that Rylee's voice rises, but he cuts us both off. "Is that understood?"

The anger in his voice stuns me momentarily, and fuck me, Rylee gets the first word in. "No way, Becks! I'm not staying in this room another second with this asshole!"

"Asshole?" It rolls of my tongue as if it's a question, but she's right. Fucking right in every sense of the word but I'm so beyond angry right now. First her and now Becks turning against me? The hairpin trigger had been pulled tight in the bar, and I'm primed and ready to fight.

I whip around to face Rylee, only to find her body fucking inches from mine. How can I hate and hurt right now but my body vibrates from her nearness? Fuck me, she's my kryptonite.

Where are the fucking superheroes now?

And I'm so grateful when she speaks because it pulls me from my thoughts—thoughts that are so fucking scattered I can't figure out which one to focus on. The woman makes me have more personalities than the splintered images of my reflection in that shattered mirror. For some reason though, I don't think all the king's horses and all the king's men will be able to put this Humpty Dumpty back together again.

She snorts in disgust. The sound forces me to focus on the here and now rather than the memories of what she feels like against me. Beneath me. Part of me.

"Yeah! Asshole!" She sneers at me with such derision that I can feel it pulse in waves off her.

Good. The wall's back up. Right where I need it to be. Fucking Christ! If she thinks that's going to hurt me, she's gonna have to try a whole fucking lot harder. It's hard to hurt a man that died inside years ago.

But I swear to God she brought me back to life.

Get your head straight, Donavan. Hurt her before she hurts you. You told her the truth. You chased. You tried. She wouldn't listen. Still isn't going to listen.

Which means she's not going to hear me. She's going to believe whatever the fuck she wants to. And in turn she's going to leave me.

Broken.

Shattered.

Irreparable.

Break her before she'll break me.

"You want to talk about assholes? Try that stunt you pulled with bar-boy back there. I believe you claimed the title right then, sweetheart."

"*Bar-boy?* Wow, because having a harmless drink is so much worse than you with your gaggle of whores earlier, right?"

She shoves at my chest like she did downstairs and I accept her anger. I welcome the physicality that comes with the force of the push. I welcome the sting in my heart from that goddamn look in her eyes that says she hates me, loves me, is hurt by me.

I need a fucking minute, a pit stop second. I need to stop that burn in my gut and get my fucking head back in the game. I pace back and forth, blowing out a breath to shove the emotion aside and bury it down deep with the rest of my secrets.

I notice the smirk on Becks's face out of the corner of my eye—the one telling me I'm in so fucking deep and the cement's starting to harden around my feet ... and around my heart—and I can't help the words that fly out of my mouth. "She's driving me fucking crazy!"

I'm talking to Beckett, friend to friend, searching for some kind of help here to quiet the confliction within and of course Rylee latches on to the one word I leave hanging out there for her like a checkered flag in the wind.

"You'd know all about the *fucking part* seeing as you fucking

Tawny is what started this whole thing in the first place," she screams at me.

I don't even have time to register the jolt of Beckett's body beside me before he stutters out, "*What?*"

Oh fuck.

"What? He didn't tell you?" She sneers at him.

Shut the fuck up, Rylee. Becks is in big brother mode and this is my fucking business.

Motherfucker.

"I told the asshole that I loved him. He bailed as fast as he could. When I showed up at the Palisades house a couple days later, Tawny opened the door. In his T-shirt. Only his T-shirt." She takes a deep breath, focused completely on Beckett and ignoring me. "Colton didn't have much more on either. Told me nothing happened. But that's a little hard to believe with his notorious reputation. Oh and the condom wrapper in his pocket."

I cringe, her words hitting every part of me that wants to hide. Becks turns to look at me and I can see it hitting him, lie by fucking lie. That I let this argument fester to become this because I'm so fucking stubborn that I didn't tell her the truth. I see the disbelief in his eyes and how infuriated he is in the clench of his jaw. "Are you fucking kidding me here?"

"*What?*" I can hear the confusion in her voice, but I can't look at her because I'm too focused on the look on his face.

"Leave it, Becks."

"What the fuck, man?" Here comes the bulldog. Fuckin' A. He's not going to leave this alone, is he?

"I'm warning you, Beckett. Stay out of this!" I'm so pissed at myself—at everything that's happened tonight—the anger inside ignites and I turn the inferno toward him. My fists clench. My blood boils.

He takes the bait, focusing on me rather than Rylee, and adds kerosene to my fire. "When you start jeopardizing my team and the race tomorrow, then it becomes my business …" He shakes his head. "Tell her!"

"Tell me what?" Rylee shouts out in the silence of the room. The only other sound is the testosterone reverberating between Becks and me.

He gives me the look—that look that tells me he is so disappointed in me, mixed with *what the fuck are you trying to pull*. I give him the only answer I can because right now I don't even know what I'm fucking doing. "Beckett, she's like talking to a goddamn brick wall. What good will it do?"

"She's right. You're an ass!" he says, and I can see the challenge in his eyes even before he spits out his next words. "You won't tell her? Fine! Then I will!"

I'm done, trigger pulled, buttons pushed successfully.

My hands grip his shirt and I'm pressing him against the wall without a second thought, jaw clenched, fists itching. "I said leave it, Becks!"

What the fuck am I doing? About to go to blows with my best friend over a fucking chick? She must be the real deal. Fucking voodoo pussy, my ass. More like schizophrenic pussy. She has me all over the goddamn place.

I can see the amusement in his eyes. The look that says, *she's got you by the balls, Wood, and I think you like it, want it, but are scared shitless.*

No fucking way.

My emotions are ruled by anger and I'm so confused my game's off and no one knows that better than him. He could have our positions reversed in a millisecond. So why hasn't he pushed back? Taken the bait? Hurt me so I'm given the due I deserve?

Instead he just lifts an eyebrow telling me to show him differently, then—show him that Rylee isn't my final rodeo—before pushing me away.

"Then fucking fix this, Colton! Fix! It!" He shouts the dare at me before yanking the hotel room door open and slamming it shut.

Unsure what to say. Not sure how to escape these confines—from feeling and not wanting to feel and everything in between—I cuss out a storm as I pace the room again, trying to ignore the fact that Ry is watching my every movement—dissecting it and trying to draw conclusions I don't want her to form. If she's not going to believe me when I told her nothing happened, then she'll never trust me anyway.

How could she really believe I'd want something more when I have her? Perfection. Necessity. The Holy motherfucking Grail.

Does she know how much it kills me that she thinks I'd do that to her? Rips my fucking gut to shreds. I've given more of myself to her than anybody else I've ever met and she doesn't trust me? My poison has tainted her now and I can't let it continue to any further. I want to punch something—need to desperately—to get rid of this overload of shit coursing through my body.

"What was that all about?" Her voice cuts through the haze, but I'm so angry I push it away, keep walking trying to calm the fuck down before I say something I'll regret. "Damn it, Colton! What don't you want me to know?"

She blocks my path and as much as I want to physically pick her up and move her out of the way so I can wear a hole in the fucking carpet until I can think rationally, I can't. I want to touch her so bad. Take her. Hold her. Accept her.

But I can't.

… no one will ever be able to love you …

She doesn't trust me.

… you're horrible and disgusting and poisoned inside …

She's going to leave me.

… you're like a toxin that will kill them …

Shatter me.

… I'm the only one that is ever allowed to love you …

Break me.

… you're worthless, Colty …

I can do worse and she can do better.

Let her go.

Push her away.

Save her.

"You really want to know?" I shout at her, hoping she flees and runs at the question but knowing not in a million years that she will. "You really want to know?"

She stands on her tiptoes, those glints of violet boring into mine, daring me to confirm what she already thinks is true in her heart. "Tell me." Her voice is a quiet calm when she says it. "Are you that Goddamn chicken shit you can't fess up and just admit it? I need to hear it come out of your mouth so I can get the fuck over you and get on with my life!"

I don't know how I swallow. I don't know how I speak, but the words are out of my mouth before I know it. Walls re-erected and solitary confinement a Siren's song calling to me. *"I fucked Tawny."*

Poison spread.

Ship crashing against the treacherous ocean rocks.

Silence settles around us but I can hear the locking of the cell.

Feel the quicksand smothering my lungs.

The death of my resurrected soul.

"You coward!" she screams, hysteria bubbling up. "You goddamn fucking coward!"

"Coward?" I shout. Does she have any fucking clue I'm trying to save her? Trying to push her away before I can fuck this up even further? Fuck her over any further? Trying to stem the sudden feeling of need? "Coward?" I ask, trying to cover up every emotion that wants to pour out of my mouth and make this even worse. I'll take the pain, but fuck me if I don't want her to know that I tried to tell her. That I tried and she ignored.

Get your head on straight, Donavan. You either want her or you don't. Decide. Figure it out because this cerebral war is fucking killing you.

Turn it back on her.

"What about you? You're so fucking stubborn that you've had the truth staring you in the face for three fucking weeks. You're up there so high and mighty on your goddamn horse you think you know everything! Well you don't, Rylee! *You don't know shit!*"

"I don't know shit? Really, Ace? *Really?*" The quiet calm in her voice scares me. Does her lack of fight mean she's over me? Fuck, no. "Well how's this? I know a bastard when I see one."

Self preservation wins.

"Been called worse by better, sweetheart." I'm not sure if the words are meant as a challenge or a coup de grace. Will she fight for me or flee while she can?

I know my answer in the flash of her hand aiming for my face. Her wrists collide into my hands without a thought, our bodies crashing together with the motion, our lips inches apart. And I'm fucking frozen. Paralyzed in that space of time where I immediately take back everything I said, everything I did, and just crave the simplicity of her addictive taste.

Just want it to be her and me back in front of that mirror. Just want to be man enough and not fucked-up enough that when she says those words to me, I don't cringe. I don't feel the blackness swallow me whole and smother the air in my lungs, but rather look in her eyes and smile.

Accept.

Reciprocate.

Love.

Her voice breaks through my haze of regret. "If you were done with me … had your fill of me … you could have just told me!" Hurt fills her eyes and trembles across her lips.

And now that I've done it—now that I've pushed her away and hurt her with my callous comments—all I want is her back in my arms, my life, at my side. Because done with her? Does she really think that?

As if a single taste of her will ever be enough.

"I'll never have my fill of you." I say the words but see the disbelief still warring in her eyes so I give into the ache. Show her the only way that I know how. Search for the balm to soothe my aching soul and the bleach to purify my blackened heart.

My mouth slants over hers. Takes and tastes and demands. I accept her struggle, accept the fact that she hates me because I hate myself too, but I can feel the need vibrate between us. Can sense that this hunger will never be satisfied. That I'll never want it to.

She keeps struggling, keeps wanting to hurt me. And I want to tell her to do just that. Hurt me like I deserve. Hurt and love are equivalent to me. The only way I know that love is supposed to be.

But I see it in her eyes. The pain I've caused. And yet I still feel the love from her. Still feel like she wants this. Wants me. And even despite all of this … all of the hurt and confusion and spiteful words we spit at each other, I want her desperately. Have to have her desperately.

And I plan to take. I have to get us back to where we were. Where we need to be. To the only place my soul has felt at peace over the past twenty-odd years.

Back to Rylee.

"You want rough, Rylee?" And despite the contempt in her eyes, I do the only thing I know how to reclaim her. "I'll give you rough!"

My lips connect with hers and I do the only thing I can: I take what I want so desperately. What's mine.

To save myself.

CRASHING INTO LOVE,
RACING TOWARD FOREVER

Crashed

BOOK THREE

K. BROMBERG

NEW YORK TIMES BESTSELLING AUTHOR

Crashed

Chapter Twelve

This chapter was originally written completely in Colton's point of view (the scene below), but after some discussion with my beta readers, I decided that using Colton's voice here took away from the impact in the next chapter. I rewrote the scene through Rylee's eyes and published that instead.

I explain this scene to people as the little boy inside the damaged man chapter. Colton breaks my heart here. He's recovering from the accident but knows no matter how extreme that pain was, it won't hold a candle to the hurt he'll feel when he pushes Rylee away. He gets it now, gets that he not only wants her, but needs her too, and yet he's trying to protect her.

You may have read this one before in the Crash D.A.S.H. posts.

THE TURBULENCE JARS ME AWAKE. Scares the fuck out of me really, seeing as I was having that damn dream again about the crash—the dream where I can't remember shit except for the dizzying, sickening feeling in the pit of my stomach and the out of control feeling in my head. Add to that the jolt of the plane, and my mile-high wake up is a hell of a lot more stressful that the one I'd really like to have with Ry.

God, how badly do I want to take that for a ride. I'm fucking hard as a rock as I've been for the past three days when I wake up but one, doctor's fucking orders. Two, we're constantly surrounded by other people, and three, after overhearing her conversation with Haddie the other night when she thought I was asleep, how can I touch her when all I'm going to do is end up hurting her.

I don't want to do that to her. Don't want her to live life always waiting for the worst to happen. I don't mind the car, don't mind what a crash could possibly do to me because the shit I lived through was much more painful than hitting a concrete barrier.

Impact can kill your body.

What my mom did to me killed my soul.

I shake the shit from my head and lift it up from the chair Ry insisted I adjust to recline. I look around to see Nurse Ratchet, the hospital approved medic sent to monitor my flight home, sit up at attention when she notices that I'm awake.

Leave me the fuck alone.

I've had enough prodding fingers and concerned eyes looking at me to last a fucking lifetime. Oh and then there were the fucking ludicrous sponge baths. Grown men sure as fuck are not supposed to have someone wash their nuts unless it's to be followed by a blowjob in the shower. On a bed with a sponge? *Fucking ridiculous.*

Good riddance to the hospital and its torturous type of solitary confinement.

Nurse Ratchet starts to unbuckle her seatbelt, and I just shake my head to tell her that I'm fine. I lie back down, angling my head to the right so I can stare at the sight across the aisle from me. Rylee's sound asleep, curled up on her side so she's facing me, no doubt so that she can watch and make sure that I'm okay.

The fucking self-sacrificing saint.

And I know she's exhausted. She misses the boys desperately despite being on the phone with them every chance she gets. Add to that the nightmares she's been having every night that wake me, allowing me to be the silent witness to the fucking agony I'm inflicting upon her. She shouts out Max's name. My name. Begs for us to live. Begs to take our place so she can die instead. Begs for me not to race again.

Screams for a car to stop and let me out. And I know this because I lie awake holding her while she trembles in her sleep. Holding her—holding on to her as I breathe in everything I can—so that I can live with the ghost of her when I finally bring myself to do what I need to do.

Be selfless for the first time in my life.

And the time has come.

Way too soon—forever would be too fucking soon—but it has come.

And the thought has every single fucking part of me protesting over the gut-wrenching hurt that's to come. That I'll be inflicting on myself. Pain I'm sure that will be a thousand times worse than these ear-splitting headaches that come and go on a fucking whim, because this kind will be from tearing myself apart, not from trying to put myself back together.

Humpty fuckin' Dumpty.

She sighs softly, shifting in her sleep, and a curl falls over her cheek. I give into the need—the one that is so inherent now that I'm fucking scared to death of how I'll be able to lessen it in the coming days—reach out and move it off of her face. I curse my fucking fingers as they tremble from the after effects of what we still hope is just swelling. They stop shaking and so I let them linger, enjoying the feel of her skin against my fingertips.

What the fuck is going on with me? How is it I fought my whole life to not need, *to not feel* ... and now that I do, I'll gladly take the pain so she doesn't have to?

But the thought I can't shake keeps tumbling through my obviously screwed-up head. If she's my fucking pleasure, how in the hell am I going to bury the pain when I push her away? From pushing her away? I shake my head, unsure, and welcome the stab of pain from the action because it's got nothing on what's going to happen to my heart.

But there's no other option. Especially after overhearing her on the phone with Haddie last night when she thought I was asleep. Hysterical hiccupping sobs. Denials of how she's ever going to watch me get in a car again. Hearing the brutal reality of what she went through killed me, fucking ripped me to shreds as I lie with my back to her, remorse hardening my heart, tears burning my eyes, and guilt submerging my soul. Learning that her abrupt trips out of my hospital room are so she can throw up because she's so sick with worry over it. How she's eating Tums like candy to lessen the constant acid eating through her stomach from my need to return to the track. How she'll support me, urge me, help me get back in the car, but will have to sneak out before the pace car is off the lead lap. How she won't be able to hear the sounds and see the sights without replaying the images that are etched in her mind. Won't be able to look me in the eyes and wish me luck without thinking she's sending me to my death.

A shiver of recourse revolts through my body.

And then there's the other hint that I'm getting from her—that I can see in her eyes when she shifts them away—that tells me she knows something I don't. She has one of my memories and is holding it hostage. But which fucking one?

The hints swirl of what I've lost in the black abyss of my mind. Ghosts of memories converge, overlapping and all shouting for attention at once. They scream at me like fans asking for autographs—all begging for attention—faceless, nameless people all wanting something—yelling at the tops of their lungs—and yet all I hear is white noise.

All I see is a blur of mixed color.

Why is it I can still remember the shit that stains my soul but I can't seem to remember the bleach I've found that washes it away? And I have a feeling that whatever Rylee is guarding is that important. That monumental. She wouldn't be keeping it from me unless she was trying to protect me. Or her.

But from what?

In my dreams I hear her saying she can't do this anymore. Is that it? Is she going to end this? Is she going to walk away and never look back? Break me into a million fucking pieces?

What the fuck, Donavan? You're going to do it to her. Walk away to save her from yourself. And you think it's going to be any easier just because you're doing it? Think that the acid-laced knife that's going to barb through your heart is going to hurt any less because it's by your own hand?

Fucking crash.

Goddamn prescriptions that I swear are messing up my head.

Fucking voodoo pussy.

My fucking Rylee.

I watch her. Can't move my eyes away from those thick lashes on cream-colored skin. Over her all-consuming lips and down over the swell of her tits. She's arms' length away but I still know how she smells. How she tastes and sounds and feels. It will forever be embedded in my mind.

Irremovable.

Irreplaceable.

Yeah, my dick stirs to life—it's Rylee, isn't it? But so much more stirs and swells and hopes that I don't even fight the tears welling in my eyes. For the second time in more years than I can count, I let the tears fall. Silent tracks of impending devastation staining my face.

Who knew that doing what was right for someone else could feel so incredibly wrong? Could break the strongest man by weakening his heart?

Will reduce me to nothing?

I know she can give me what I need—quiet the demons in my head that torment my soul and parasitic heart—like the adrenaline of losing myself in the blur at the track, but I can't do that to her. I can't in good conscience hold on to her so tightly in order to lose my demons when it's causing hers to invade her sleep. I can't take the pleasure when it's causing her all of the pain.

Before, I could. I would have. But this is Rylee here. The selfless soul who means too fucking much to me. So, no I can't.

Not now.

Not ever to Rylee.

It feels so good to let it all out—the confusion, the loss of hope, the dying of my redemption—yet hurts so badly as the tears fight their way out and scorch my face. Singe my soul. Crumble possibilities.

I squeeze my eyes shut and try to shut out the memories that I do have. The ones flickering like a strobe light through the haze of my time with Rylee. The tears turn to silent sobs and eventually even those dissipate into hitching breaths.

When I open my eyes, violet pools of concern are staring at me with a mix of confusion and sympathy. "Colton?"

Fuck. I don't want her to see me like this. Remember me like this. Some pussified man bawling his eyes out for reasons she can't fathom.

I can hear the worry in her voice but all her face shows is compassion, understanding, acceptance. And that makes what I have to say so much harder. The words are there on the tip of my tongue and I fool myself into believing that I'm about to say them.

Acid on my taste buds.

Bile in my throat.

The fracturing of my heart.

She reaches out and cups her hand to the side of my face, her thumb wiping away the stains—just like her heart has brushed away vile memories—and a soft smile ghosts her mouth.

I race you, Rylee.

The words feather through my mind and another tear slips over.

And I've never felt more exposed in my life.

Guard down.

Heart open.

Soul needing.

Accepting.

Wanting.

I'm so fucking lost right now. Lost even though I've been found. Even though she's found me.

And I get it now. Get why she can't watch me get in the car again. Get why she'd be so selfless—encourage, push, help—even when it's killing her. Breaking inside while pretending on the outside that she's whole.

But I'm nowhere near okay.

Not going to be for a long time.

If ever again.

I open my mouth but I can't bring myself to do it. I can't bring myself to tell her this isn't what she deserves. That I'm not what she deserves. That I could do so much worse—have done so much worse—and she can do so much better. That I understand she can't go through this again. I'm not sure how to. I try to force the words off my tongue but they die, self-preservation at its finest. Silence is my only option. The only way to quell the guilt that eats at me every time she looks in my eyes and gives me the same soft smile she's giving me now.

She has to be wondering why I'm crying. Why I'm being such a chick, but she doesn't ask. Instead, she sits up slowly and looks around the private jet before rising and closing the distance between us. She gives me a look as if she's asking if it's okay and before I can even answer, she's settling in my lap, nuzzling her head under my chin, wrapping her arms around me as best she can.

The soothing balm to my aching soul.

She doesn't say a word, but just holds on, easing whatever she thinks is wrong with me by her mere presence. And of course now the tears well again like a fucking broken faucet and I hate it. Hate myself right now.

And I am so wrong.

I thought I could live with the pain—manage—but holy shit I feel as if my body is broken—fucking shattered into a million pieces, and I haven't even told her yet. Haven't even taken a step away but holy mother of God, I'm already knocked to my knees.

Already struggling to breathe when the air is cocooning me.

It's time to hit the concrete barrier head on without a seat belt, without my lifeline.

How in the fuck am I going to do this?

Crashed

Chapter Fourteen

The almost but not quite sex scene in CRASHED. The racing term sex scene. Whatever you want to refer to it as, this was an often requested scene to read in Colton's point of view.

He's had this big accident, pushed Rylee away earlier in the night, and yet he wakes up and here she still is. She's scared and he's scarred and yet she's still fighting.

It was fun and challenging writing this chapter from a male perspective. I had the constant fear I was making him sound too soft, too hard (no pun intended here, ladies … I'm talking about emotion—*emotion here*—get your minds out of the gutter), too crass, or not crass enough. I think I nailed it (ha, couldn't resist), hope you think so too.

… *DRAGONS LIVE FOREVER, BUT NOT so little boys* …

The lyrics filter into my head, my own dragons—and not the playful, puffy kinds—are front and fucking center, but that's not the problem. The problem is I'm not a little boy and yet I'm still living with this shit.

I slowly ease awake and can't believe how nice it feels with her arms wrapped around me instead of that soul-jarring, mind-fucked moment when you wake up alone with only your demons lurking in the dark corners to keep you company.

I close my eyes for a second, accepting that she's still here after everything I've put her through.

"My dad used to sing that to me when I had nightmares."

Her body jolts at the sound of my voice as I put my arm around her and pull her closer, skin to skin. My own personal balm to coat the inked reminders on my torso that reflect the stains on my soul.

"I know," she whispers, "and you were."

I press a kiss to the top of her head and leave my mouth there, breathing her in. Trying to wash the dream from my mind. Needing to.

I think of how I'd much rather dream about the crash than *him*. How almost dying, going headfirst into a wall, is ten times easier to cope with than the smell of the musty mattress, the feel of his hands on me, the taste of anticipatory fear.

I need to talk, to scavenge some of the thoughts from within and release them so I can start to breathe again. I pick the one she knows the most about, the one that won't make her look at me and think I'm weak for succumbing to its clutches.

"I was scared. I remember the vague sense of being scared those last few seconds in the car as I was flipping through the air." I don't know why that's so hard to admit to her.

She runs her hand over my chest. "I was too."

"I know," I say evenly but hate myself for putting her in that position. Loathe that she fears anything because of me. I reach down, my hand sliding beneath the band of her panties to cup the curve of her ass and pull her up so she can look into my eyes. I hate rehashing shit, but I owe her this ten times over and then some. "I'm sorry you had to go through that again."

Her eyes glisten with tears and now I hate that I've made her cry bringing it up, but when she leans forward and brushes her lips against mine, all thoughts are lost but one.

Take.

And hell if it's the emotion of the day, needing to erase my dreams, or simply being so fucking relieved to be alive, but I do just that.

I squeeze her ass in my hands so her tits rub up against me, and every part of my body begs, craves, and is starved for more of her. I need to hear that sigh she makes, need her taste on my tongue, and I don't hesitate. I slip my tongue between her lips and don't even realize the groan is coming from me.

Thank fuck I survived the crash because I need this little slice of Heaven right now, and I sure as shit know this was going to be one of the first things I'd miss if I'd died and landed in Hell.

I bring my free hand to her face and slide my other one from her ass up her back and put them in my favorite place tangled in her curls so she has no other option but to open up to me. And when I pull her head back, I see just that in her eyes: vulnerability, need, and desire all balled into one dick hardening look.

Hell, I was hard before that, but shit, there's no turning back now.

"Ry, I …" My mind fires, fleeting flashes of stolen thoughts but none stick against the wall. Things I want to say flicker and fade just as quick as they come, but the feeling within me remains burning bright. I clear my throat, trying to buy time for them to come out but nothing does so I say the only thing I can. "Thank you for staying."

Fuck this. That's not what I want to say. Man the fuck up, Donavan. You told her if you can't say it, you'll show her any way you can. So fucking show her.

"There's nowhere else I'd rather be," she says, snapping me from my conflicting thoughts. I meet her eyes, a man on a mission now. Wanting to take and needing to prove.

My hand pisses me the fuck off because I want to lift her up and onto me so I can keep my head still and not trigger another goddamn headache and ruin this, but it's not working. And fuck do I need it to work more than ever right now. But Ry anticipates what I want, so she straddles my hips and looks down at me.

I take her all in, lips parted, nipples hard beneath her tank, and the fucking heat of her pussy on my very desperate cock. Desire ignites between us and within moments our lips are on one another's, hands touching, bodies aching for so much more than this.

My good hand grips onto her hip, urging her to rock like that again over my dick and when she does, fuckin' A. All thoughts flee because my mind and body are in total agreement on what they want: *her*. Any way I can get her because it's been so fucking long since I've buried myself in her addictive pussy.

My right hand moves to her other hip because I need my woman naked right now. Need to see her tits, rub my thumbs over her nipples for my own fucking pleasure and hers. I'm so lost in the taste of her kiss that when I go to grip her tank top, I forget about my hand—that it can't pull the fabric up and over her head.

Without missing a beat, Rylee comes to the rescue—like always—and has the shirt off. And fuck I've seen her tits before but don't think I've ever wanted her more than right now.

Screw what the doctor says, what my head is going to feel like, because this man is not waiting. No fucking way when she is sitting like this atop me. Vixen, siren, mine. The last one mattering the most.

Her mouth meets mine again, her tits against my chest. My hand on her hip guides her to slide over my boxer-brief clad cock, making me ache in the worst way, in the best way. And when she moans and sits back up, I fight every primal instinct in me to flip her over and fuck her into oblivion. She is the epitome of sex right now and all I want to do is taste, take, and sate my desire.

I lean up, the slight twinge of pain in my head drowned out by the desire owning my body, and take the tip of her tit into my mouth. Her cool flesh against my warm tongue only adds to the riotous frenzy within me.

I flick my tongue over her nipple and claim her mouth again while my right hand lamely palms her breast. I know the minute she feels my hand's fucked-up grip because she brings her hands to mine, laces her fingers with them, and moves them to her hips.

I groan as she drags her lips from my mouth and leans her forehead against mine, dreading and knowing what she's going to say.

"We can't. It's not safe."

We can. Fuck safety. Fuck any reason you're going to deny me because I'm not ashamed to admit I'm a desperate man willing to break every rule to have you.

"It's too much exertion," she explains.

"Baby, if I'm not exerting myself, then I'm sure as fuck not doing it right." I can't help but chuckle against that spot on her neck. I feel goose bumps across her skin as I rub my stubble against it to let the flash of pain in my head abate.

Her nipples press into my chest and I know she sits up to fight her own urge to take and fuck if that doesn't make her even sexier. But even better is she positions herself perfectly so that my dick presses against the damp spot on her panties. Her lips part and eyes close momentarily as I purposely adjust my hips, pushing my cock against our double cloth barrier into the dent of her pussy. I get a low groan but I want more from her. I want to hear her tell me to take her.

"*Colton,*" she moans and fuck, saying my name like that is like my own personal verbal Viagra. There's no way I'm turning back now because then both heads will be throbbing in pain.

"You know you don't want me to stop," I say, hoping she's willing to break a few rules, but she reaches out and places her finger on my lips to quiet me

"*This woman* is just trying to keep you safe." Her voice has that husky rasp to it that tells me she's fighting this just as hard as I am. And damn her restraint is a challenge I can't wait to test.

Game on, baby.

"Oh, but you forget that the patient is always right and *this patient* thinks that *this woman,*" I say as I open my mouth and suck on her finger, swirl my tongue around it, eyes locked on hers, "needs to be thoroughly fucked by this man."

She squeezes my hips with her knees, and I can feel her control slipping, my dick pulsing against her. Almost there, baby.

"Safety," she reiterates with unwavering resolve and fuck, I thought she was closer to caving than this. Time to bring out the big guns. Well the big guns beside the one she's sitting astride rubbing herself against right now.

"Ryles, when have you ever known me to play it safe? Please … let me exert myself," I plead, flashing her that no-holds-barred grin of mine. The one that she's told me makes her wet because it means I'm about to take her. But fuck if my voice isn't strained from the painful ache in my balls. I roll my hips again, and this time she grinds down at the same time so she's testing more than just my control, she's testing my sanity too. I lick my lips and look at her, eyes taunting, dick teasing. "I'm dying to take the driver's seat and set the pace."

K. BROMBERG

Her laugh fills the room and I just look at her, confused to why the hazy look in her eyes has been replaced with humor. What the fuck, Ry? This is not a laughing fucking matter.

"When we first met, Haddie wondered if you fucked like you drive."

Talk about shifting gears when the only one I want to be shifting is into her … but her comment finally makes its way through my pussy-possessed mind and I can't help but laugh at Haddie's question. Hmm. Wonder how she answered.

"And how's that?"

"A little reckless, pushing all the limits, and in it until the very last lap …" she says, her fingernail scraping down my chest causing my balls to tighten and priming every muscle in my body to pounce.

But I hold myself back, know she's playing some kind of game here. I can see it in her eyes, and I'm torn between letting it play out and giving in to fucking her senseless.

I angle my head to the side and stare at her. I love when feisty Rylee comes out to play, so fuck yes I'll accept the painful ache drawing this out will cause me.

I'll play the game all right, follow her lead, but she better be ready to let me win this round when all is said and done. A man has only so much restraint after all.

"Well, was she right or do I need to take you for another spin around the track to refresh your memory?"

You gonna say no, sweetheart? I love the look on her face, love that I caught her off guard. Tell me, show me, what's flickering through those eyes of yours.

Our eyes lock for a moment as I try to read what she's thinking but fuck if I can hold them there when her fingers slide over my happy trail and then up over the scant excuse she's wearing for panties.

And then they sit there. Taunting me. They move slightly over the waistband like she's as desperate to touch herself as I am.

"Not sure I remember, Ace. It's been a while since I've seen you in action."

This is the game she's playing? Drive me crazy? Fuckin' A, measure me for the straight jacket because I'm sure we could put it to some kind of kinky use.

I don't think she has any clue how much she owns me right now.

Fucking owns every single part of me and doesn't have a damn clue. Sitting astride me, fingers atop the little piece of Heaven that I'd die to claim right now, and the sarcastic dare falling from her mouth. My mind wanders to what exactly those fingers would look like nestled between those folds of flesh, and I have to stifle the groan at how fucking hot the vision is. And I think that's exactly what she's trying to do—tease me with what she won't give me. With what I can't claim yet.

She wants to play, huh? Oh, I am so fucking game right now. Ready to knock it out of the goddamn park.

"Baby, if you're trying to get me to stop, then you shouldn't throw around comments like that." I shift in the bed and *accidentally* roll my hips again, feeding into the pleasurable pain as my aching cock rubs against her tempting pussy yet again. And this time I know I've hit her right where it counts because she throws her head back and the soft sigh that falls from her mouth is a dead giveaway no matter how unaffected she's trying to play it.

I can't take my eyes off of her. The sight of her tits, weighted globes of perfection, right in front of my face. I force my eyes to move upwards and meet the challenge in hers. "If you think I fuck like I drive, you should see me drop the hammer and *race* you to the finish line."

I see her breath catch and her body stutter in its motion momentarily before she quickly recovers and regains her composure. My mind starts to try and figure what I just missed but my thoughts are pulled out from underneath me when she spreads her legs apart further, the wetness on her panties spreading wider. My fingers rub together, itching to touch.

"I thought racing wasn't a team sport," she says coyly. "You know, more of an *every man for himself* kind of thing." Her eyes hold mine as her fingers slip beneath the band of her red silken panties and still, my eyes darting between the two waiting for her to move them. Begging her to move them. The visual consuming my thoughts.

I force myself to look away, to work a swallow in my throat that's suddenly become dry. "Every man, yes," I finally am able to get out. "It can be very dangerous too, you know?"

"Oh really?" she asks, eyes locked on mine, the moan of pleasure that falls from her lips has my breath laboring as I look down to watch the movement of her fingers beneath the fabric in front of me.

"*Sweet Jesus!*" I can't handle the unknown, needing to see for myself the show on display. And thank fuck my right hand decides to work when I need it most because the fragile fabric of her panties is snapped and dropped in an instant without a second thought.

And Rylee doesn't even skip a beat.

Oh fucking my. The white French tips of her nails are a mind-dizzying contrast to the darkened pink flesh they dance across. Perfection. Addiction. Absolution. I glance up knowing she's going to have that taunting smile on her lips and for the second time in as many seconds I'm knocked breathless.

Fucking kryptonite.

Rylee's head is thrown back, curls tumbling all over the place, lips parted, tits pushed out, and the sexiest moan coming from her lips as she doesn't just revel in the moment but becomes the fucking moment. *Fuck me.* The woman who used to tighten the sheet around her months ago in modesty now sits astride me in all of her glory, owning her body and sexuality with such a confidence that I've never thought her to be more sexy, more sensual, more everything than right now.

She lifts her head forward, her hand sliding out from between her legs, moisture glistening off of her fingers for me to see. "Well, Ace, danger can be overrated. It seems I know how to handle a *slick track* perfectly well." She smirks that smug smile I want to fuck off her face right now just before she slips her arousal coated fingers into her mouth and sucks on them, eyes taunting me all the while.

Is she trying to kill me right now? Fucking voodoo pussy is back with a vengeance and fuck if I'm not ready to be the first and only victim. The woman has me strung tighter than a hair string trigger—volatile and ready to blow. My balls tighten, my body tenses wanting her so desperately, but my stubborn streak tells me I have to hold out, take the reins when the time is right. My body screams that time was ten fucking minutes ago, while my head loves when Ry gets feisty and defiant. When she makes me work for it like no one else ever has.

"Slippery and wet, huh? Danger has never been more fucking tempting," I tell her, my eyes watching as she pulls her fingers from between her very fuckable lips and follows the descent back down south. She adds torment to her tantalization by parting her seam with one hand so I can more than handily see her other fingers add the friction her sighs say is more than pleasurable.

Fuck me this is brutal to watch and not partake in when all I want to do is urge her hips closer to my face and have her sweet taste on my tongue again. For that alone, it's time for me to mess with her a little more and knock her out of the pleasure inducing coma that's darkening the violet in her eyes.

"You know, sometimes in a race, in order to reach the finish line, rookies like you have to tag team to get the result you want."

Her head snaps up, lips parting, and eyes flashing with shock momentarily until she regains her composure. Perfect. Threw you there didn't I, sweetheart?

"Sorry, but this engine seems to be doing just fine running solo." She smirks at me, so arrogant that she thinks she dodged the proverbial bullet. Too bad I'm holding the only gun allowed to shoot that shell. And fuck me, she's sliding her hands back down to my place between her thighs, her moan of pleasure when she finds purchase—my own personal Heaven and Hell.

And then she stops and looks at me, lust in her eyes and evidence of her arousal on her hands. "I know exactly what it's going to take to get me to the finish line."

"Oh, so you like to race dirty, huh? Break all the rules?" I ask, fingers trailing up her thighs, leaving visible goose bumps in their wake, her body angling toward me the higher I go. Fuckin' A straight. She can play the aloof card all she wants but she can't deny that her body readily submits to me when I want it to. And fuck, how I want it to right now.

"Oh, I most definitely can handle dirty," she taunts as she trails a finger up my chest and rubs some of her moisture across my lips. My tongue darts out, unable to resist the temptation to taste what I'm craving and fuck me if it doesn't make me want to flip her over, cuff her hands over her head, and fuck the defiance out of her until she's screaming my name and owning my heart more than she already does.

She grinds her hips down, that smarmy smile still teasing the corners of her mouth as she rocks back and forth over me. She leans forward, her breath a taunting whisper against my ear. "Being a seasoned pro such as yourself, you just might have to show this rookie exactly why they say rubbing's racing."

She's playing the temptress card and passing with flying fucking colors. I don't even have time to recover from the notion that her pussy's wetness is starting to soak through my boxer-briefs when she rocks her hips again. I try to remain unaffected, play her game, but I have to grit my teeth to prevent my eyes from closing at the rocket of sensation that just shot through me.

When I look from her hand back up to her eyes, she raises her eyebrows in the final coup de grace. "Big bad professional race car driver like you afraid to show a newbie how to drive stick, huh?"

And I can't take it anymore. Fuse lit and control shot. Within a beat, I've pushed her back up to sitting, pulled her feet flat on the bed beside my ribs and knees spread wide, because if I'm watching the feature presentation, I better have a goddamn front row seat.

"I'm shifting gears, sweetheart, because I'm the only one allowed to drive this car." My hands slide up again until they reach the juncture of her thighs. My thumbs brush over her tight strip of curls before I readjust and tuck my fingers into her. She cries out, her tight walls flexing around me and milking against my fingers as they stroke the nerves within. And between her wetness on my fingers and the memories of her gripping my dick has me pre-coming like a fucking adolescent school boy but fuck me, I'll take it. I'll take anything I can from her because Rylee? *She's fucking everything.*

She doesn't take long to climb because she's so addled with pent up need—and the fact that it's only for me is not lost in the frenzied moment. Her fingernails score my skin, body tenses, and pussy convulses as the broken cry of my name fills the room around us.

My name moaning from her lips. God-fucking-damn is that not the sexiest sound I've ever heard.

I give her a moment to gain her breath, the senses I've just finger-fucked out of her, and when I think she's coherent enough, I let her know that even though she's just come, I'm the one who just won the race.

"Hey, rookie?"

She lifts her head forward and looks at me from beneath weighted eyelids heavy with satisfaction. "Hmm?" is all she can manage and I fucking love that drowsy just-been-fucked-right look on her face. The one that only I can put there.

"I'm the only one that's allowed to drive you to the motherfucking checkered flag."

She just throws her head back and laughs, cheeks flushed, tits jiggling.

Fucking gorgeous.

Like I said, she's everything.

The Holy motherfucking Grail.

Crashed

Chapter Twenty-Two

What was Colton thinking the first time he stepped back in the car after the accident? He's pushed Rylee away because of the bullshit Tawny has laid at his doorstep, he received a dress down from his dad the night before, and now he has to face the one demon he can to gain back the freedom he needs to outrun his other ones on the track.

And he has to do it without Rylee, the one person he desperately wants to be there.

Or does he?

Fear is a brutal bitch to face.

It squeezes your lungs so you can't breathe, locks your jaw to bear the brunt of your stress, and cinches your heart so your blood rushes through your body.

The guys are at my back pretending to be busy. Ignoring the fact that I'm standing in front of my car, staring at the cause of my biggest fucking fear right now and my greatest goddamn salvation. I need it more than ever between the bullshit Tawny hit me with and not having the one person I want most but don't want to taint any further around.

Rylee.

She said she'd be here when I got in the car for the first time. I need her here, need to know she's here to come back to at the end of the run. The salve to my stained soul. But how in the fuck could I call her and ask her when I've pushed her so far away?

So here I stand, surrounded by my crew but battling the shit in my head all alone. And of course my mind veers to the vultures at the gates that shoved cameras in my face and spewed Tawny's bullshit lies about Rylee when I left the house earlier. Then it slides back to Rylee and how much I want her here right now.

Fuck this, Donavan. Quit being such a pussy and get in the god-damn car. You've faced shit ten times worse than this. You've got this. Man the fuck up and get in the car.

I take a deep breath and squeeze my eyes shut momentarily as I lift my helmet and push it down on my head. My silent acknowledgement to the guys that I'm ready to tackle this.

It takes me a minute to buckle my helmet; my hands tremble like a motherfucker. Becks steps forward to help and I glare at him to back the fuck off. If I can't fasten this then I don't deserve to get behind the wheel.

I slide my hand up the nose toward the cockpit. I knock softly out of habit to ease my superstitious mind.

Spiderman. Batman. Superman. Ironman.

Four knocks, one for each of the superheroes that the little boy in me still thinks will help protect him. They pulled me through the last crash, I know they're good for it.

I take a deep breath and try not to think as I lift one leg and then the other so I can drop into the driver's seat. I sit there, try to make myself numb so I can't feel the fear coursing through me and trickling down the line of my spine in rivulets of sweat.

Becks steps up and locks the steering wheel in place and thank fuck for that because now I have somewhere I can put my hands and grip so that they stop shaking. I feel his hand pat the top of my helmet like he usually does, but before he clicks my HANS device he pulls my helmet up so I'm forced to look at him.

I see the fear flicker in his eyes but I also see resolve. "All you,

Wood. Take your time. Ease into her." He nods at me. "Just like riding a bike."

A bike my ass. But I nod at him because I have a feeling I could argue the point just to cause a distraction from actually having to do this. I focus on the wheel in front of me as he studies me, gauging whether I really am okay being here.

"I'm good," I lie. And he stands there for a minute more before the guys bring the crank out and we fire the engine.

The reverberation through my body and sound in my ears of the engine's rumble is like coming home and making me question myself all at once. Kind of like Rylee.

I hold onto that thought—to the idea of her being here when she's not—as I rev the motor a few times. It sounds the same and yet so very different from the memory still hit and miss in my mind from the wreck.

The crew gets over the wall and it's just Becks and me. He leans over and pulls on my harness, the same way he has for the past fourteen years. It's comforting in a sense because he doesn't act like anything is different, knows that this is what I need. Routine. The sense that everything is the same when it's a clusterfuck in my head.

He raps the hood twice as is his habit and walks away. I don't follow him because if I do, I know I'll see the falter in his step. And his hesitancy will reaffirm my fear that I'm not ready.

I give it some gas, let the car rumble all around me to clear my head, and psych myself to do this. And I sit here long enough that I know I look like a pussy who shouldn't be in the car so I put the car in gear and begin to ease out onto pit row. My heart is in my throat and my body vibrates from more than just the car. Nerves and anxiety collide with the need to be here, to do this, to be able to outrun my demons and find the freedom-laced solace I've always been able to find on the track.

I exit pit row and squeeze the wheel, frustrated that my fucking grandmother can drive faster than I am.

"That's it, Wood. Nice and easy," Becks says, and it takes everything I have to shut him out, to listen to the car like I always do and try and hear what she's telling me. But I can't drown out the bullshit in my head so I close my eyes momentarily and tell myself to just push the gas and go.

And I do. I push it, flick the paddle as I change gears, and enter the high line into turn two because I'm not going fast enough to have to worry about drifting into the wall.

But the more I accelerate, the less I hear. She's not talking to me. The noises aren't the same. "Goddammit, Becks! This car is shit! I thought you checked everything. It's—"

"Nothing's wrong with the car, Colton."

"*Bullshit!* It's shuddering like a bitch and is gonna come apart once I open her up," I grate out, pissed at that placating tone in his voice. I'm the one in the fucking car—the one that can possibly slam headfirst into the wall—not him.

"It's a new car. I checked every inch of it."

"You don't know what the fuck you're talking about, Beckett! Goddammit!" I pound my fist against the steering wheel, completely backing off the gas.

I know he says something about taking it nice and easy but I don't really hear it because the flashback hits me so hard I suffocate in the open air.

The car stops but dizziness spirals through me.

My body slams to a stop but my head hasn't.

A breath shocks into me as I realize what just happened. That I survived that tumbling pirouette into the catch fence. That I escaped the shredded fucking mass of metal on the track at my back.

Pain radiates around me like a motherfucking freight train. My head splinters into a million damn pieces, hands grabbing and groping and pushing and prodding. That familiar pang twists in my gut because I don't want anyone's hands on me, can't handle the feeling. I don't want to be reminded of the little boy I used to be and the fear that used to course through me when I was touched by others. *By him.*

Medical jargon flies at a rapid pace and it's so technical I can't catch the gist. Just tell me if I'm going to be fucking all right. Just tell me if I'm dead or alive, because I swear to God my life really did just flash before my eyes and what I thought was going to be … what I thought I wanted out of life … just got twisted and turned more than the aluminum of my car.

How could I have been so wrong? How could I have thought change would be the catalyst when it ended up being my fucking epiphany? Shows me to try and change the road fate's already set for me.

I writhe to get away from the hands that touch, twisting and turning to find her. To go back and tell her that I was so wrong. Everything I put her through. Each rejection and rebuff was my fault. Was a huge mistake.

How do I make it right again?

Pain grapples again and mixes with the fear that ripples under the surface. My head feels like it is going to explode. Lazy clouds of haze float in and out and eat the memories away. Take them with them as they leave and fade. Darkness overcomes the edges until I can't take it anymore. Voices shout and hands assess my injuries, but I fade.

My thoughts.

My past.

My life.

Bit by bit.

Piece by piece.

Until I am cloaked in the cover of darkness.

"Colton?" It's her voice that shocks me from my memory like a drowning man finally breaking the surface for air. I gasp in a breath just as hungrily.

I shake my head and look around. I'm all alone on the backstretch of the track, sweat soaking through my fire suit. Did I really hear Ry or was that part of my flashback?

"Rylee?" I call her name. I don't care that there are guys on the mics that probably think I'm losing it because she's not here ... because they're right. I am losing it.

"Talk to me. Tell me what's going through your head. No one's on the radio but you and me."

She's here. It's her. I don't even know what to do because I feel like I'm hit with a wave of emotions. Relief, fear, anxiety, need.

"Ry ... I can't ... I don't think I can ..." I'm such a fucking head case that I can't string my thoughts together to finish a thought.

"You can do this," she tells me like she actually believes it, because

I sure as fuck don't. "This is California, Colton, not Florida. There's no traffic. No rookie drivers to make stupid mistakes. No smoke you can't see through. No wreck to drive into. It's just you and me, Colton. You and me, nothing but sheets."

Those words. I know they don't belong right here in this moment but fuck if they don't draw a sliver of a laugh from my mouth but that's all I can manage because they also make me think of everything I've put her through. How nothing but sheets between us has led to her having to deal with the fallout of Tawny and all of that bullshit.

And yet somehow she's here. She came for me. Does she have any fucking clue what that means to me especially when I'm the last one on earth that deserves her right now?

I pushed and now she's pulling.

"I just …" Can't do this anymore. Push you away and hurt you. Push the gas and drive the car. Not have you near me.

I know my head's fucked up but I'm in overload mode again and then she speaks and lets light into my darkness.

"You can do this, Colton. We can do this together, okay? I'm right here. I'm not going anywhere."

I don't deserve you. Your faith in me. Your belief in me.

"Are your hands on the wheel?" The confidence in her voice staggers me when I feel anything but.

"Mmm-hmm … but my right hand—"

"Is perfectly okay. I've seen you use it," she says and the thought flickers through my head of just how she saw it the last time we had sex.

"Is your foot on the pedal?" she asks.

"Ry?" I want to stay in these thoughts of her, don't want the fear to ride the wave back into my psyche.

"Pedal. Yes or no?"

"Yes …" *But I'm not sure I can do this.*

"Okay, clear your head. It's just you and the track, Ace. You can do this. You need this. It's your freedom, remember?"

She knows the words to pull me back from the edge. I take a deep breath and hold on to the confidence that she has to try and override the fear crippling my thoughts with images and sensations of tumbling into the wall. The wall that looks exactly like the one to the right of me.

Surrounding me.

C'mon, Donavan. Engage the motor. Prevent it from dying. The engine revs and a part of me sighs at the progress.

"You know this like the back of your hand … push down on the gas. Flick the paddle and press down."

I make myself focus on her voice, hold on to the thought that she came back to help fix the broken in me. And the car starts to move down the backstretch and into turn three.

"Okay … see? You've got this. You don't have to go fast. It's a new car, it's going to feel different. Becks will be pissed if you burn up the engine anyway so take it slow."

I push a little harder, accelerator unsteady, but I'm starting to move around the track. I pass the point similar to where I went into the wall in St. Petersburg and I force my mind to tune out the unease and focus on listening to the car talk to me.

"You okay?" I can't answer her because I may be trying to engage mentally but my body is still owned by the fear. "Talk to me, Colton. I'm right here."

"My hands won't stop shaking," I tell her as I look at the gauges and realize I'm going faster. And with speed I need to concentrate on the feeling of the track beneath me, the pull of the wheel one way or another, the camber when I hit the corners. Routine items I can diagnose without thinking. Because I don't want to think. Then doubts come, fear creeps.

I shake the thought and sigh, knowing how much shit I'm going to get from Becks since I'm not focusing like I should on the task at hand. "Becks is gonna be pissed because my head's fucked-up."

She doesn't respond and I start to crawl back in my own mind for a moment when she clears her throat. She has my attention now. Is she crying?

"It's okay … watching you out there? Mine is fucked-up too … but you're ready. You can do this." Something about her willingness to be vulnerable to me when I know she's standing around all the guys hits places inside I'm glad I can't analyze right now.

"Aren't we a fucking pair?" I laugh, finding it rather humorous how screwed up we both are.

"We are indeed," she says, and the little laugh she emits tells me so much. I press the accelerator down some. I've never needed approval from anyone, but right now I need it from her. Need her to see that I'm trying, both on and off the track.

"Hey, Ace, can I bring the guys back on?"

"Yeah," I reply quickly. I hit turn four again and feel a little more confident, a lot more sure that I can do this. And I know how a large part of that is because she's here. Shit, even after I was an asshole to her, have put her through hell with the paparazzi chasing her, she's still here. "Ry … I …" My voice fades but my mind completes them.

I'm sorry.

I race you.

Thank you.

"I know, Colton. Me too." Her voice breaks when she says it, and I feel like I can breathe again, like my world was just somehow set right when it's been inside out the time without her.

Crashed

Chapter Forty-One and a Half

Colton's demons have robbed him of so much in his life. But he's finally faced them, finally told Rylee he loves her. We know how the story ends, so when did he have that *a-ha* moment when he knew she was the one he wanted to do the one thing he swore he'd never do—*get married*?

In this new scene, you'll get the answers.

SHE SWITCHED IT. WHEN THE hell did she do that?

I pick up the picture from my bookshelf, the one that sits in exactly the same place the one of Tawny and me used to. Frame's the same, picture's not.

The new one is of Ry and me at my comeback race. I don't fight the smirk when I think that wasn't the only victory lane I claimed that night with her arms wrapped around my waist.

And something else around my cock.

Fuck, she's gorgeous. Her head is angled back, grin on her face, but her eyes are on me. And that look in them—that frozen moment of time—reflects clear as fucking day her feelings for me. Not a single doubt.

I'm one lucky son of a bitch.

Well shit. When I look at my image, there's no denying I feel the same way about her. The look on my ugly mug tells anyone who sees the picture that she's snagged me hook, line, and double-sinker.

Funny thing is I see a man completely voodooed and I'm not even spooked by it.

I'm still getting used to the thought of it, the taste of it. And hell if I'm quite liking the foreign feeling, especially because it means I get to slide between those sexy as fuck curves of hers and claim the finish line every chance I get.

I know the game has caught up with this player because as much as that thought's a turn on, I like the idea even more that when I wake up I can reach over to find her in my bed next to me, that sleepy smile on her lips and that rasp to her morning voice.

God, I sound like a fucking pussy. All sappy and shit.

The woman has topped me from the bottom when I never thought it was a possibility. But fuck me, being beneath her means I get a damn good view of those tits of hers while I'm looking up.

My balls tighten at the thought alone.

Yep. I'm a damn voodooed man. Who would've known it'd feel so good to be under a woman's spell.

I'm starting to feel cracks in the ground beneath me because Hell sure as fuck is starting to freeze over.

I set the picture down, glancing one more time at it with a shake of my head. Nice, Ry. A sly removal of Tawny and subtle claiming of me.

And fuck if I don't like that claim. Who would've thought? Huh. Stranger fucking things have happened over the past few months I shouldn't be so shocked by feeling so okay with this.

Those baby steps of mine have turned into full on leaps. I guess I should start practicing for the long jump if this shit keeps up.

I wander out of the office forgetting the article from *Race Weekly*, so completely lost in thought. And then I see the woman who holds them captive. She's out on the patio in deep discussion with my mom and Quinlan over something.

And it's fucking weird how perfectly she fits here, there, everywhere in my life.

Jesus, I sound like a fucking Dr. Seuss poem.

"How come you're not at the track?"

My dad's voice pulls me from my thoughts, and I immediately realize I forgot to grab the article for him, distracted by Ry's bait and switch. And then I wonder how long he's been standing there watching me watch Rylee.

"What? Why would I be at the track?" He's lost me. It's Sunday, a non-race day and no testing scheduled, so why the fuck would I be at the track?

He looks me in the eyes like he always has to judge how I'm doing from what he sees there since talking's not really my forte. And for the first time in forever, he gets this ghost of a smirk and just nods his head like he knows something I don't. He stares at me a moment longer and then hands me the bottle of beer in his hand before sitting down in one of two leather chairs facing the fine-ass view in front of us.

Of the ocean and the women.

"Sit down, son."

Famous fucking last words. I suddenly feel like I'm thirteen again and about to get read the riot act for something or other that I most likely deserve to get punished for. I take a pull on the beer, enjoying my last meal before the sentence is handed down.

I sigh and plop down next to him and repeat my question. "Why would I be at the track?"

"Because that's where you go when you need to think things through."

I look over at him like he's lost it because he sure as fuck is losing me. "Is there something you know that I don't? Like what exactly I'm supposed to be thinking through?"

"You know life is one big scavenger hunt," he says before falling silent. I stare at him as he looks out the window and try to follow the bread crumbs he seems to be dropping here. "Fate hands you a list of things to experience. Ones you never expected, ones that break you, ones that heal you. So many of them you swear you'll never even attempt or want to cross off your list. You get caught up in the day to day, moment to moment, and then one day you look at your list and realize you've unexpectedly completed some of the tasks. It's only then you realize that the brutal truths the scavenger hunt has made you face has not only made you a better person, but has also given you an unforeseen prize when all is finally said and done."

Has he been hitting the bottle today when I didn't know? He's gone from the track to a scavenger hunt. I get he's talking about my life in some context, but I need help connecting the dots here.

"Dad." I sigh the word, part question, part exasperation. Throw me a goddamn bone here.

Rylee laughs and the sound floats inside causing me to look back at her.

Always back to her.

"I'm not going to lie, your list has had some pretty fucked-up shit on it, son."

The way he says it, like he blames himself for the shit he couldn't prevent, stabs at the parts deep inside of me. Parts I'd always thought dead until recently. The kid in me starts to apologize and then I stop myself. Can't apologize if I don't know what the fuck I did wrong, so I just sip my beer and give a noncommittal sound, not wanting him to feel guilty for the demons that came before he could protect me.

"I just think it's time that you look at your list. Take stock of all of those things—expected and unexpected—and look at what extra things you've earned for crossing those items off."

Silence falls between us as his words and what I think they mean start to sink in. The weight that has been lifted from my shoulders. The poison exorcised from my soul. The new chance at life without the demons snipping at my heels.

All because of the defiant as fuck contradiction of a woman my eyes keep drifting back to.

"Sinner and saint," I murmur without thought. My dad either doesn't hear me because he just pulls the beer to his lips and takes another sip or chooses to let my comment slide. And as thoughts connect, puzzle pieces begin to fall in place. "Dad?"

"Hmm?" He doesn't look at me, just keeps his eyes forward when I slide a glance his way.

"What is it you think I'm thinking about?" My voice doesn't sound like mine when I ask it. It's cautious, quiet, and I don't care because all I want to know is his answer.

"How you're going to ask Rylee to marry you."

He delivers the statement so matter-of-factly that it takes a moment for me to register that I'm choking out, "Fucking Christ, Dad!"

Disbelieving laughter follows right behind my words. I scrub my hands over my face, more than aware of his scrutiny, and yet my mind races with his comment. Parts way down deep that I'm not sure I want to acknowledge flutter to life like nerves right before the green flag is waved on race day. Nerves that tell me my adrenaline need is about to get its next fix.

A fix.

A necessity.

Something you can't fucking live without.

Rylee.

Dots connected. Bread crumbs scattered and gone so I can't find my way back again.

The question is, do I want to?

Shit, I've got Becks chewing my ear about it and now my old man starting in. Fuck yes, the thought has crossed my mind. But shit I just realized I'm capable of loving someone, let's not shoot the gun without loading it first.

Ruin a good thing by fucking it up with something that's so bad for so many.

And things are good between us. Like fucking stellar. We've never talked marriage. Never even brought the word up. I told her I wanted to see what life hands us and she was cool with that. Didn't say first comes marriage and shit.

So why all a sudden is the idea mulling around in my head when it's a finish line I swore I was never going to officially cross.

Fuck me running. C'mon, Donavan. Speak the fuck up. Assert yourself. Say hell no instead of wondering what it would feel like to have her name be Rylee Donavan.

"Well, I don't hear you saying no, now do I?" He glances my way, raises his eyebrows, and then leans back to put his feet up on the coffee table.

Ah fuck, he's getting comfortable. I know what this means.

Can't we just back the hell up here? I prefer the guessing game. I can fill in another answer we can get stuck on. Anything but this be-cause it's causing me to think of things I shouldn't be thinking.

I pinch the bridge of my nose and squeeze my eyes shut momen-tarily as I try to wish the conversation away. And when I do, all I see is that goddamn vision of Rylee in a white dress that Becks's com-ments at the pool party caused me to think of. And shit, that vision comes back with a vengeance. Veils and rings and shit I shouldn't be thinking of. Shit that's getting way too comfortable as a visitor in my thoughts lately.

I shake my head. Need to clear this nonsense. Rid it of the road this man is never going to race down. So why do I see the metaphor-ical finish line at the end of the track all of a sudden?

My heart pounds momentarily until I push away the thoughts his words are creating. What the fuck is going on here? Why does my dad have me thinking of scavenger hunts and marriage proposals? *Sweet Jesus.*

"You're not pulling any punches today, are you?"

"I don't believe I threw one," he says, completely unaffected.

Is he fucking kidding me? Must be nice to sit there so calm and collected when he's doling out sucker punches to make a damn point.

I slump down in the chair and rest my head against the back of it, eyes looking up at the pool's reflection on the ceiling. I focus on it as he allows me the silence I need to swish the thoughts around like mouthwash. A necessary evil that burns before it leaves you cleansed.

Marriage.

The word lingers. There's something about it that I can't quite put my finger on. First causing panic, then banging around like a ping pong ball before feeling like that fucking grain of sand in my swim trunks. The one you feel at first, irritating with every movement—your mind thinking of how you need to strip your suit off so you can wash it out—but then as minutes pass to hours, you don't feel it anymore.

It's still there, in that spot right between your nuts and your thigh, and you're kind of okay with it.

And it's all because of her.

Fucking Rylee. I shake my head, one thought more than all oth-ers front and center. With temerity and defiance, obstinance and patience, she chipped away at every hard edge of me until there was nothing left but the truths I feared. The bent and broken. The ones buried so goddamn deep I knew they'd push her away.

And yet when all was said and done, when the poison in my soul was lying on the table so she could see how fucking dark it was, she looked me in the eyes and told me I was brave, loved the broken in me. I gave her my darkest and her response was to give me her light. Her love.

I blow out another sigh and scrub my hand over my face, words forming and then dying before I can speak.

"C'mon, Dad, me? Marry someone?" I spit the words out—words that used to be a given fact—so why in the fuck do they feel like lies when they come from my mouth while I'm looking at her?

"I call bullshit. Nice try though."

And there's the knock-out punch.

I stare at him, waiting for him to look at me, wanting the fight to prove he's wrong. To prove that nothing's changed. I can be with Rylee but that's enough for me. No rings, no strings.

But that half-ass smirk is the only reaction he'll give me to the buttons of mine he's pushing with expertise. One by fucking one.

So why doesn't that pitching feeling in my stomach come when I think of it all of a sudden? I have so many fucking excuses why I'll never get married and yet even with the last push of my button, not a single one comes to mind.

The only thing that does cross my mind is the woman sitting feet away, well within perfect reach.

"Life only hands you so many chances, Son. You seem to have used quite a few this year already. I don't think you should take many more for granted." He turns his head now and locks eyes with mine. The man that's sat beside me most in my life, held my hand to help me conquer my biggest fears, called my superheroes with me, is telling me there's one left I have yet to face.

That there's one item left on my scavenger hunt that will give me an even bigger reward than I ever thought I deserved or was imaginable.

Something happens.

Fuck if I can explain it other than that dead calm right before the green flag waves. When your body is amped up on adrenaline, mind is blanking sound out, everything is happening at a lightning-fast speed, but you sit there like time is in slow motion. Calm. Resolute.

At peace.

I force a swallow down my throat, past my heart lodged there, because motherfucker … this broken man who was once held together with Scotch tape is now rock solid, and it's all because of Rylee.

She may be my kryptonite but fuck if I'm the superhero worthy of her.

His words echo in my head. Pushing me. Questioning me. Making me want things I never expected to want or deserve. Ever. I look down at the label, my fingers playing idly with it as ideas form, possibilities arise.

"How did you know Mom was the one?" I don't give him a yes or no answer that my thoughts just might be veering in the direction his questions ask me about. I keep my head down, needing to get used to this idea myself.

Let the grain of sand irritating my nuts become a bit more familiar first.

I can feel his eyes on me, know he wants me to look up at him, but I can't. Fucking sand isn't all that comfortable just yet.

"How did I know?" He chuckles and the tone of his voice has a corner of my mouth pulling up into a smile. "Your mother walked into the cafeteria on the lot one day. She was an extra and I was an assistant director and she intimidated the hell out of me. She was gorgeous and commanded attention. And then she looked up and smiled at me and I knew. Just like that." He pauses for a beat until I raise my eyes to meet his.

"How did I know? Because I let her in, let her see the good, bad, and ugly about me. I gave your mother the power to destroy me when I fell in love with her, and she didn't. She was my prize at the end of my scavenger hunt. Without her I wouldn't have this," he says, motioning to my sister and then me. He glances out to my mom and smiles softly before looking back at me. "In racing terms, she was my checkered flag, Son."

… I gave her the power to destroy me …

His words stagger me. Open me. Urge me. Seal a fate I never had control of until now.

He has no idea I call Rylee my checkered flag—no fucking clue—so I'm knocked back a pit stop second, pulse pounding, mind thinking of possibilities that were never mine to think.

I'm so focused on my thoughts and the bottle of beer in my hand, I jump when he cuffs me on the shoulder. "You'll figure it out, Colton. You'll make the right decision when or if you want to." He rises from the chair and stands there looking outside for a moment. "You're a good man. She'd be lucky to have you, just like your mom and I have been."

He starts to walk away, his unending confidence in me still staggering after all this time, after all the shit I've put him through.

Even at my darkest.

"Dad." I don't know why I stop him when the conversation itself has made me uncomfortable, but I do.

He stops but doesn't turn around, his back to me.

Words tumble. Thoughts scramble. But for some reason the ones that never stuck before are the only ones that do now.

"I love you." The words are out without thought, my hands shaking, the little boy in me hoping he hears them.

I immediately hear the hitch of his breath as his whole body freezes. He slowly hangs his head forward, his shoulders shuddering momentarily. He raises his head and nods a couple of times. "And that is my unexpected reward for my scavenger hunt." His voice is thick with emotion. "I love you too, Son." He says it so softly before waiting a beat and walking into the kitchen area.

I exhale the breath I was holding, thankful he didn't make a big deal and embarrass me when he heard the words it's taken me a lifetime to say. Grateful we're so close that he knows what I needed.

I shake my head. Shit, that was intense. All of it. Revelations and confessions I never expected to make all of a sudden fall like rain around me.

Fuckin' A.

I look up and Rylee's eyes lock with mine. The smile comes so naturally to her lips that my body—head and heart—react immediately to her.

And I know.

Just like that.

Something I've spent a lifetime fighting is all of a sudden knocked out by this defiant as fuck woman who owns the heart she showed me could beat again.

Fuck me. I just keep knocking 'em down one right after the other. Might as well tackle this bad boy while I'm on a roll.

My mind starts churning, ideas forming. The scavenger hunt of my life continues. I smile back at her as I stand and just stare.

My future.

My salvation.

The woman I want to marry.

Fuck. That grain of sand just became comfortable.

I guess the plus side is if marriage is sand, at least I know my dick is going to be covered in it.

Crashed

Chapter Forty-Four

The number one most requested scene of all the books. What a wedding looks like through Colton's eyes.

I LOOK AT MYSELF IN the mirror, my thoughts a jumble of shit but my pulse steady, body calm. I shake my head.

Life is such a mindfuck sometimes.

The man I see looking back at me is not the same one I would have found a year or even six months ago.

It's like each fucking day with her makes me a better person. A better man. Erases some of the demons bit by bit, moment by moment.

I splash some water on my face, the disbelief still riding high that I'm about to get fucking married. Me? Colton fucking Donavan. The self-proclaimed bachelor for life. The man who thought no pussy is good enough to want for a lifetime.

Fuck! I laugh into the empty bathroom. Talk about underestimating the power of voodoo.

How naïve I was. Always needing to mask the pain and hide the scars on my soul by burying myself in the next willing piece of ass. Never—never—did I think this day would come. That I'd wake up wanting a woman in bed with me and not just beneath me.

Fucking Rylee.

The woman knocked me on my ass like a three hundred pound linebacker. Talk about blindsiding my way of fucking life filled with tits, ass, Jack and Jim, and thinking only about myself.

Because now all I can think about is her.

Even now.

Right fucking now I should be hung over, puking my guts out with nerves over the ball and chain about to get shackled to my ankle. But fuck if I feel any of that. All I want is to see her. Kiss her. Make her mine in every way.

Ride off into the proverbial motherfucking sunset.

And all of this because I got schooled by Becks into understanding why the *alphabet* is so damn important. A to fucking Z of it.

"Dude, you gonna finish getting ready or what?"

Becks's voice startles me. I glance down to my phone where Ry's last text is on the screen still—**I'll be the one in white**—to check the time and realize shit's about to get real.

"Hold your horses, Daniels." I lift my chin in acknowledgement to him through my reflection as I bring the tumbler of aged Macallan he bought for the occasion to my lips. "I'm just zipping up now."

"Don't pinch your dick. You just might need that tonight since she's been holding out on you." He chuckles as he pours himself a glass.

"No shit." I tuck my shirt in, my mind wandering to just what's going to be beneath her dress besides my voodoo pussy. Because fuck if it's not torture to sleep beside the woman you want more than the air you breathe when she won't let you touch her. "A month is a long fucking time, dude." I groan the words out, my dick already stirring for the action it's been missing.

He throws his head back and laughs at me. "For you that's like a lifetime."

"Fuck off." He just raises his eyebrows at me, then I can't help but laugh. "It's been brutal."

"Poor baby. You'll get no sympathy from me. Welcome to how

the other half lives, where snapping your fingers doesn't result in any woman you want dropping to her knees."

I laugh. "Not anymore, brother. Not anymore." I'm on the please remain standing program now. I glance up from where I'm trying to put my checkered flag cuff links through the holes to meet his eyes.

"You really ready to do this?" He quirks his eyebrows up at me, like he's waiting for the about face. For me to freak the hell out because I'm about to get hitched.

He's fucking crazy if he thinks I'm walking away from Rylee. Not now. Not ever. That checkered flag's only ever going to wave for me.

"I should be nervous right? Pacing and shit. But I'm not. Fucking scary but true … *it's Rylee*," I tell him with a shrug as if that it explains it all. The thought unnerving even to me.

But fuck if I've been able to make sense of the truths she's allowed me to face, the man she's given me the room to become.

"It is indeed Rylee, and shit, man, I don't know what she sees in you," he teases, "but, she looks incredible."

What? "You've seen her?" So not fucking fair. So many things I want to ask him about her, but I keep my balls and retain my dignity. I'll see for myself soon enough if she's nervous or smiling or crying.

Being beautiful is a given.

"Had to talk to her, let her understand the big ass mistake she's about to make … give her a chance to ride off in the sunset with the more handsome of the two of us."

I snort out a laugh as I walk toward him. "Yep. We will be doing that in about six hours. Thanks for showing her the lesser so she knows she's getting the more."

"Cocky as fuck and you still end up with the girl."

"Always." I sit down on the edge of the chair across from him and flash him an arrogant-ass grin. And fuck if I know where it comes from but all of a sudden there are so many things I need to say to him and not enough words to say them with. We may fuck with each other, ride each other's asses when we can't see what's right in front of us, but I know the shove he gave me knocking my dick in the dirt is part of the reason I got my shit together. Is why I'm sitting here right now, about to marry the girl I sure as shit don't deserve.

Well him and the defiant as fuck woman who grabbed me by the balls and said non-negotiable.

"Hey, Becks?"

"What do you need?"

And that right there gets me. His unwavering friendship.

I look down for a moment and take a sip of the Macallan. "That's good shit. Thanks," I say, stalling.

"A rarity for a one-of-a-kind type of day."

Years of friendship come down to right now. Two young kids, now men, and the one that was fucked-up just might finally have it together. How the hell do I tell him that? Thanks for putting up with my bullshit and being my punching bag and wingman all at once?

"Thanks, man. *For everything*." It's all I've got, but I think he knows what I'm saying because he meets my eyes for a moment, a slight smirk on his face, and nods his head in acknowledgement.

"Always." He sips his drink and then leans forward and taps it against mine. "And just remember to always end a fight with these two words: *yes dear*. Biting your tongue at the end of a fight will up the ante of her using hers later to make-up."

I laugh with him and his fucked-up logic that makes perfect sense before tossing back the rest of my drink.

"You ready, Son?" My dad's voice from the door interrupts us.

I sigh and fuck if I can't stop the smile that's on my face. "Yep, just putting my tie on," I say, rising to get it. I meet my dad's eyes and we had our father-son moment earlier but I still can't get over that look he gives me.

The pride mixed with attaboy. The look the fucked-up little boy I was would have killed to have as much as something to eat and yet here I am, twenty something years later, and it means more now than I ever thought it could.

Sweet Jesus. When people say weddings make you sappy, they weren't fucking kidding. But fuck anyone who tells me I don't deserve this. I've been to Hell and back, survived the darkest shit imaginable and I'm standing here with my old man and my best friend about to marry the woman who took the pieces the poison hadn't eaten through and made me whole again.

I think I need another drink.

Let's get this waiting shit over.

I'm restless. Antsy as fuck. I mean, I'm close to all of the people here but they seriously need to stop chatting and sit the hell down so I can see her.

"Cool your jets. You've waited this long, I don't think another couple of minutes will kill you."

Her voice startles me but I keep my eyes focused on all of the guests. "Easy for you to say," I tell my sister, knowing it's no use to bullshit her that the nerves are starting to kick in.

"Well it's about time," she says sarcastically, her hand dusting something off the shoulder of my jacket.

I glance over at her. "Exactly my point. It's about time for it to start."

"That's not what I meant." She snorts in amusement. "I meant it's about time you're finally acting normal about this. That your nerves are showing. You were freaking me out with the Mr. Cool-Calm-and-Collected routine. I wanted to ask who stole my brother."

I roll my eyes at her, my patience wearing out but for all the right reasons. When I meet her gaze I see the tears there, accept the love in them. I just sigh and shake my head, an unsteady grin on my face. "I'm getting married, Q."

A tear leaks over and she runs her hands up and down my lapels. "I know. It's surprising as hell but you deserve it. All of the happiness and love she brings you." She steps up on her toes and kisses my cheek. "Just treat her like you treated me, minus the nuggies and wedgies," she says with a wink, emotion breaking her voice, "and you'll be just fine."

I pull her into me and kiss the side of her cheek. She bats me away so I don't mess up her makeup or hair. "Thanks."

She just nods her head at me before shaking it. "I won't believe it until I see a ring on your finger." She laughs. "I guess now would be a good time to tell her parents that our family has a no return policy on you."

"Quinlan," I warn her, but the smile on my face gives away that I don't care if she tells them that or not because they won't need to return me. I'm in this for the long haul.

She's called from my mother upstairs and she kisses my cheek one last time before running up the steps.

Time passes slower than the pace car around the track. I'm amped up, ready to get the show on the road, and a new Mrs. Donavan into bed when all is said and done. The officiate leads me outside. I stand there and make eye contact with my mom who has been a wreck all day since we had breakfast until now.

The music starts. Some classical shit that I'm sure I'll never remember but at the same time will know every time I hear it what it means. Where I was. What she looked like.

Tanner and Quinlan walk down. Then Becks and Haddie. I don't even see them. I'm rocking on my heels. Clasping my hands in front of me. Telling myself to breathe.

Fuck. I'm really doing this. Really *want* to do this.

The wedding march starts. At least I know this song. Kind of hard to miss.

But when the music starts, I feel like the bottom drops out.

All of my insecurities, fears, worries begin to overtake me. I strain to find Rylee around the curve of the guests. I want to yell at them to sit the hell down so I can see her because I'm fucking suffocating and she's my air. My next breath.

My fucking everything.

And then life zooms in 3D fashion when I catch the first glimpse of her.

The blur around me stops.

All I see is white. Can't tell you a goddamn thing about the dress except for the color because all I'm focused on is her face.

Look up.

Look at me, Ryles.

I want to shout the words to her. Let her know I'm here, waiting. But then realize she can take all the time in the fucking world because I'm not going anywhere.

Yep. This man who loved to run is firmly rooted in place. Fuckin'A.

I can't hear my mom sobbing, can't feel the breeze of the ocean, can't hear the music anymore because Rylee looks up.

And I'm lost. Staggered. Found. Saved.

To her. To the moment. For the rest of my life.

My saint. The words run through my head as I lock eyes with her. Every demon left within leaves with the exhale of my breath I didn't realize I was holding.

Her smile is unwavering and eyes fill with tears as she walks so calmly toward me. And thank fuck for that. Thank God she never listened when I warned her off of me. Because it may have been a great view of her ass walking away, but that means I'd never have the chance to see this—accept this—know this feeling. The one that she's walking toward me, no secrets hidden, all slates wiped clean, and a future to build together.

I'm a lucky fucking bastard.

I breathe in, my chest aching, and when the oxygen hits my lungs I'm able to think a little clearer. My eyes obey the command to take in the whole package, take a chance to remember this one moment for the rest of my life.

And then I see it.

I laugh out loud—can't help myself—when I see the checkered flag wrapped around her waist. Only Rylee would do this for me. Add something as an ode to the significance of our checkered past and of her being my checkered flag.

I can't keep my eyes off of her. She's everything right now. Fucking everything.

I shake her dad's hand and vaguely hear his kind words because all I see is her.

"Nice checkered flag," I tell her with a laugh when all I want to do is kiss her. I feel like it's been weeks since we have, but it's been less than twenty-four hours. Pathetic but true as fuck.

"I was afraid you wouldn't know which one I was," she says, referring to her text as I take her hands in mine.

And now I feel like I can breathe again, feel like myself again because Rylee's right where she belongs. "Baby, I'd know where you are even if I were blind."

I smile at her, see so many things in those eyes of hers that I don't even realize the officiate has begun. And fuck if the nerves aren't beginning to hum now.

The vows I had planned to say all jumble in my head, crossing lines and not making any sense. I hear my cue and in the split second decide that this self-proclaimed player is going to do something a year ago I would have hidden from.

I decide to let it all out. Speak from the heart. Lay it on the line so she has no doubts.

"Rylee," I say, shaking my head and looking down at our hands, calling to my superheroes asking for help to not fuck this up, before looking back up at her. "I was a man racing through life, the idea of love never crossing my radar. It just wasn't for me. And then you *crashed* into my life. You saw good in me when I didn't. You saw possibility when I saw nothing. When I pushed you away, you pushed back ten times harder." I close my eyes momentarily, a nervous laugh falling from my lips as I hope she understands how important that is to me. How she never gave up on me. Ever.

I squeeze her hands as so many emotions fill me. I have to clear my throat to continue. "You showed me your heart, time and again. You taught me checkered flags are so much more valuable off the track than on. You brought light to my darkness with your selflessness, your temerity ..." The tears start falling down her cheeks and I know they're from joy but I have to brush them away.

"You've given me a life I never even knew I wanted, Ry. And for that? I promise to give myself to you—the broken, the bent, and every piece in between—wholeheartedly, without deception, without outside influences. I promise to text you songs to make you hear me when you just won't listen. I promise to encourage your compassion because that's what makes you, you. I promise to push you to be spontaneous because breaking rules is what I do best," I say, trying to smile at her as it all catches up with me—the moment, the meaning, the woman willing to accept me—and I can't help the tear that falls when I try to blink it away. I need something funny here, something to make her laugh so the sound of it will make me more at ease. "I promise to play lots and lots of baseball, making sure we touch each base. *Home run!*"

She laughs and I breathe a sigh of relief knowing I'll be able to make it through the rest of what I have to say and that I won't fuck them up. That I've got this.

"And that right there … that laugh? I promise to make you laugh like that every single day. *And sigh.* I like hearing your sighs too." God that blush on her cheeks makes me want to take her upstairs and put it there from exertion. Soon, Donavan. Soon.

"I promise nothing will be more valuable in my life than you. That you will never be inconsequential. That those you love, I'll love too." I look over toward the boys, knowing how important it is to acknowledge them. To let them know that they are part of this package deal too. "As I stand here promising to be yours, to give you all of me, I already know that a lifetime will never be long enough to love you. It's just not possible. But, baby, I've got forever to try, if you'll have me."

My last words tumble out. Hope I said everything I'm supposed to say in a set of vows but don't really care if I didn't because Rylee heard. She gets me.

I pull the ring from my pocket and slide it on her trembling fingers. And the sight of my ring, the diamond band against her engagement ring, sends an adrenaline rush through me. Fills me with a pride I've never known and don't think I can explain.

She chokes out a yes and I think I say I love you. Scratch that. I know I did, but it's all a blur because I realize that it's my turn to listen. To be put on the hot spot because fuck if it's not easier to say the words than it is to hear them, accept them, believe them.

Earn them.

And then she touches my cheek and motherfucker … her hand on my face makes every ounce of testosterone in my body beg to take her. I glance over at the person marrying us, giving her the *help a brother out* look, to see if I can kiss her but am met with a deadpan expression.

And as much as I want her lips on mine, I can wait. This moment means too much to me and I'll have the rest of my life to kiss Rylee.

Among other things. And hell if that's not a great fucking motivating thought to keep my hands to myself right now.

"Colton, as much as I tried to fight it, I think I've been in love with you since I fell out of that storage closet and crashed into your arms. *A chance encounter.* You saw a spark in me when all I'd felt for so long was grief. You showed me romance when you swore it wasn't real. You taught me I deserve to feel when all I'd been for so long was numb." Her voice is shaky at first and then she evens it out and it's so goddamn sexy—that rasp in it—that I fall under her spell like I did that first night. I squeeze her hands to let her know it's okay, I'm right here. That I can't wait to listen to the rest of what she has to tell me.

"You showed me scars—inside and out—are beautiful and to own them without fear. You showed me the real you—*you let me in*—when you always shut others out. You showed me such fortitude and bravery that I had no choice but to love you. And even though you never knew it, you showed me your heart time and time again. Every bent piece of it."

If I hadn't already known what being broken felt like, I'd say those words of hers would have just shattered me, but in a good way. Because I know the difference. I'll never break when I have her by my side because she'll bend with me, hold the chips that break off when times get tough and help me put them back.

She's opened me up for all to see and now I know why she only wanted close friends of ours here instead of the massive party I suggested. She wanted me comfortable, willing to accept the fact that she just laid me wide open with her words and be okay with that, with the tears sliding down my cheeks.

The woman knows me better than I know myself.

"You say I brought light to your darkness, but I disagree. Your light was always there, I just showed you how to let it shine. You're giving me the life I've always wanted. And for that? I promise to give myself to you—the defiance, the selflessness, the whole damn alphabet—wholeheartedly, without deception, without outside influences."

I force a swallow down my throat and before I can process everything, her lips are on mine. Yep, she knows exactly what I need.

"Rule breaker," I say, wanting so much more than the tease of her taste.

"I learned from the best," she says.

There's my girl, learning how to live on the edge.

"I promise to encourage your free spirit and rule-breaking ways because that's what makes you, you. I promise to challenge you and push you so we can continue to grow into better versions of ourselves. I promise to be patient and hold your hand when you want it held the least, because that's what I do best. I promise to text you songs too so we can keep the lines of communication open between us. And I promise to wear dresses with zippers up the back."

What? She throws me but when I hear Haddie laughing and look over to her I can only begin to guess what she's told Ry. But I'll take it because a zipper up the back means she needs my hands on her to help.

And hands on her naked curves are never a bad thing.

"I promise a lifetime of laughter, ice cream breakfasts, and pancake dinners. And as much as I love waving that checkered flag? *Batter-up, baby."*

Game on. Yes, she's taken ladies and gents. This woman is one hundred percent mine.

"I promise that nothing will be more valuable in my life than you—because everything else is inconsequential—and you, Colton, are most definitely not. I remember sitting in a Starbucks watching you and wondering what it would be like to get the chance to love you, and now I get a lifetime to find out. And I still don't think that will be enough time."

I watch as Rylee slides the ring on my finger and wait for the fear to take hold. For the *what the fuck am I doing* to fill my thoughts. But there's nothing. Fucking nothing but love.

And then Becks starts coughing.

"You're next, fucker." The words are out of my mouth before I can stop them. And when I look up to meet Ry's eyes as everyone is around us laughing and she's smiling wide at me, I realize just how right I got this. Letting her in. Letting her help heal me.

Letting her love me.

"Colton, we've got forever to try, if you'll have me?"

"You know this is permanent, right?" I stare into her eyes. The ones I know narrow and glare when she's pissed at me, the ones that close halfway before rolling up when she's about to come, the ones that widen in surprise or brim with tears when she's touched, and I realize I can't wait to wake up every morning of the rest of my life and learn how else they can look at me. Fuck I'm lucky.

"I wouldn't have you any other way." I hear her suck in a breath when I glance down at my new ring and then realization hits me.

I glance over to the officiate and I don't give a fuck if she says no; I'm kissing her this time because I know the important shit is over.

Vows are said.

Rings are on.

Rylee's mine.

"Yes, Colton." She laughs at me. "You may kiss your bride!"

"Thank Christ!" My body hums and all of the sudden my adrenaline hits me when I know we're official. That I get these lips for the rest of my life. "This is one checkered flag I'm forever claiming."

I kiss her. I pour all of the words I couldn't say to tell her how I feel into it. Fuck the peck on the lips shit because this man's going in for the kill. Gotta make sure she knows on the first kiss of our married life exactly how I feel.

My actions definitely speak louder than words.

"Friends and family, may I present to you Mr. and Mrs. Colton Donavan."

The words hit my ears while my mouth is on hers and I know I've never felt more whole.

Rylee fucking Donavan.

That has one hell of a ring to it.

I kiss her again before I release her to hear that laugh I love falling from her lips.

My wife.

My life.

Thank fuck I can drive like the wind because happily ever after is waiting for us to drive into its sunset.

The End

Turn the page for an exclusive excerpt
of Slow Burn (Becks and Haddie's story)

EXCLUSIVE EXCERPT
of
SLOW BURN

"Pretty sure of yourself, aren't you?" And hell if the confidence isn't sexy on him.

"Hm. You may have said no strings, bu you most definitely didn't say anything about rope."

Damn. "You want to tie me up, then? I never thought you for that type, Becks." I try to deflect him with my comment but hell if the comment doesn't have me wanting him even more.

He laughs low and suggestive. "I might be; I might not be. What type I am doesn't matter because what does is the fact that ropes or no ropes, I plan on making you weak, making you hoarse, leaving you breathless. Baby, I can dominate with the best of them. The question here is how bad do you want it?"

Desperately.

And the volley of power resumes. The dark promise of his words leaves me wanting to relinquish the upper hand because it's no fun being at the top if there's no one underneath you.

He leans in and uses his mouth to silence my thoughts. Our mouths meet in a soft whisper of a kiss before his tongue touches the seam of my lips asking for access. I deny him, fists clenched in restraint, libido protesting my resistance, but I know if I let him kiss me, let him own my every reaction like he so mindblowingly can, I'll come undone here on the porch in a matter of seconds, my desire so tangible I feel like it's rolling off of me in waves.

I think he's going to be angry at my refusal. I can feel his fingers tense when I hold steadfast. That strained laugh of his surprises me yet again when he leans back, his eyes dancing with victory. "I call your bluff, Haddie Montgomery. You didn't come and I'm going to have so much fun proving it."

Acknowledgements

Thank you to all of those that help me make these books what they are. To Christina Hernandez, Donna Elliot, and Alison Manning: Thank you for making the day to day a little smoother and my day a little brighter. To Amy McAvoy and Cara Arthur: You'll always be a part of the craziness in my world, but I wish you the best of luck with your new endeavors. To Maxann Dobson, Stacey Blake, and Deborah Bradseth: Thanks for making my books look pretty in all ways imaginable. To Amy Tannenbaum and all the support at the Jane Rotrosen Agency: Thank you for always looking out for my best interests. To all my author friends: Thank you for answering my annoying questions, always lending an ear when I need it, and helping make sense of this craziness when I can't. To the bloggers: Without you, all of this wouldn't be possible so thank you so very much for all you do, all your support, and all of your friendship. I couldn't do this without you. To Jenny and Gitte: Thank you for asking the question *what is Colton thinking* and unknowingly changing the course of this series by challenging me to write a male point of view. To my family: Thank you for your patience and for putting up with the stress and chaos I've brought into our lives. To my readers: Words aren't enough to express my gratitude. You've changed my world and given me a purpose I never expected to have. For that I'm eternally grateful.

About the Author

New York Times and *USA Today* Bestselling author K. Bromberg writes contemporary novels that contain a mixture of sweet, emotional, a whole lot of sexy and a little bit of real. She likes to write strong heroines and damaged heroes who we love to hate and hate to love.

She's a mixture of most of her female characters: sassy, intelligent, stubborn, reserved, outgoing, driven, emotional, strong, and wears her heart on her sleeve. All of which she displays daily with her husband and three children where they live in Southern California.

On a whim, K. Bromberg decided to try her hand at this writing thing. Since then she has written **The Driven Series** (*Driven, Fueled, Crashed, Raced*), the standalone **Driven Novels** (*Slow Burn, Sweet Ache, Hard Beat* (releasing 11/3/15), and a short story titled *UnRaveled*. She is currently working on new projects and a few surprises for her readers.

She loves to hear from her readers so make sure you check her out on social media.

http://pinterest.com/kbrombergwrites/
@KBrombergDriven
@ColtonDonavan